AGENTS OF THE DESERT

D.S. Cannon

Also by D.S. Cannon

Insurgent Fire

This is a work of fiction. Names, characters, places, events and incidents are either the products of the author's imagination or used in a fictitious manner. Any resemblance to actual persons, living or dead, or actual events is purely coincidental.

For my wife, Emily. Who encouraged me to write a book and then never read it. Please read this one.

AGENTS OF THE
DESERT

PROLOGUE

October 4th, 2010

Las Vegas, Nevada

The Eiffel Tower outside the Paris Hotel and Casino in Las Vegas toppled to the ground with an earth shaking crash. The force of the blast shattered most of the windows in the hotel on the south side, sending shards of glass raining down on the few tourists who weren't vaporized by the initial blast. The plume of smoke soared into the sky darkening an otherwise sunny and cloudless day. Twisted metal girders snaked out across Las Vegas Boulevard like steel serpents slithering across the asphalt. Bodies littered the ground as people toppled from the tower restaurant. The heat from the blast scorched the concrete façade of the hotel, staining it a sooty black that made it look a hundred years older in an instant. Panic ensued on the ground as cars began to pile up on the boulevard, slamming into one another in vain attempts to dodge debris. Pedestrians scattered in every direction, trampling one another to escape to safety.

Agent Lilith Holyfield had tried to stop the van. Oh how she tried. She and Agent Bill Stanley had pursued it since it had been spotted on Interstate 15 in Arizona and called in by a plucky state trooper. Lilith was driving, with Bill riding shot-gun. As they closed the distance, the van slowed slightly allowing Lilith to close the gap even further but as she did, the back doors swung open and without any delay her black Ford Edge SUV was peppered with a stream of rounds from an assault rifle wielding man in the van. She swerved, nearly losing control as the weight of the SUV tried to roll itself over. Rounds streaked their way across the hood and up the windshield sending chips of black paint and sparks dancing into the air and over the roof. Bill was hit. He screamed as blood splattered the passenger window. The windshield was a wrecked mess of bullet holes and spider web shaped cracks that worked their way across the entire sheet of glass, doing their best to block Lilith's vision. Steam began to billow from the engine compartment through the fresh new holes. The radiator was fucked. *This is it*, Lilith thought as she stepped on the gas. The Ford's engine shrieked as it struggled to speed up. The body of the vehicle shook violently as the engine attempted to break free of its mounts like a wild horse trying to break captivity.

The Central Intelligence Agency had trained Lilith well. Very well in fact. She was as proficient at driving as she was at shooting, which was extremely. Any gun was lethal in her hands as was any vehicle if she needed it to be, and right now she needed it to be. The pedal was floored, but she pressed harder anyway trying to coax more power from the dying engine. It whined in response. Bill swore under his breath and Lilith told him it would be alright. Her eyes trained on the white van she desperately chased. "This wasn't supposed to happen this way," Bill stammered.

What did he mean this way? She told him shit happens. That he'll be alright. Visibility was nearing zero now and the engine smoke was starting to creep into the cabin. The Ford Edge was approaching the van while the man in the back reloaded his rifle. He was jerked from side to side as the van swerved around the traffic of daily commuters.

"C…Can't stop it…" Bill murmured.

"Watch me," Lilith said enthusiastically.

"No," he said, "Braden paid me…" Lilith's eyes grew wide. She asked him what the fuck he had just said. The man in the back of the van resumed firing. Bullets cracked around the Ford but the whine of the engine drowned them out. "Braden Murphy…he…" Bill began to draw the pistol on his right hip, "… his attack… will… happen."

Lilith saw the movement of Bill's arm in her peripherals and thrust her right arm out to block his arm as he drew on her. The pistol fired into the dashboard shattering the radio screen. Sparks burst into the cabin like a firework had been set off. She slammed his hand into the dash, knocking the pistol loose. It fell to the floor with a thud. She jammed her elbow into his ribs which caused him to scream in pain. Lilith was preoccupied with Bill and she didn't notice the man in the van was no longer firing at them. She also didn't notice the van had changed lanes to take the exit ramp. Bill laughed, blood flecks spraying from his mouth. Lilith turned her focus back to the road, but it was too late. The Ford slammed into the back of a Dodge minivan, caving the tailgate door in like it were made of paper. Lilith finally lost control. She crossed her arms in front of her face as the vehicle swerved to the right and flipped on its side. It smashed into the concrete barrier and spiraled over the edge, managing to complete four full flips in the air as it dove down to the service road below before coming to a rest on its passenger side.

Startled awake by the concussion of a large blast, Lilith tried to move but her seatbelt was stuck. She was pinned to her seat, her arms dangling in the air. Bill Stanley was slumped over in the passenger seat, still buckled in. His right arm had been torn off just below the elbow. Blood pooled on the concrete at the end of the stump. Lilith vomited when she saw most of his face was hanging from the dashboard. Minutes that felt like hours passed as she dipped in and out of consciousness. Her stomach pinched every time she looked at Bill. It took all the energy she had left to choke back more vomit. She barely felt it when she was being pulled from the vehicle. The only thought on her mind was how much the terrorist Braden Murphy had paid Agent Bill Stanley.

***

Lilith Holyfield stood in her Penthouse suite of the Bellagio Hotel and Casino staring out of the window at the Las Vegas Strip. Once a bustling tourist destination full of performers, celebrities and normal people alike was now nothing more than a scorch mark in the Nevada desert. Her arms folded behind her back, she scanned the horizon as the setting sun cast a faint orange glow over the Strip. Her gaze fell downward to the fallen Eiffel Tower that lay strewn across the street. The sight brought back the memories of the day she tried to stop that from happening and the money that Braden Murphy had promised to her partner Bill Stanley which she happily collected in his place. *Ten Million Dollars.* She shook her head slowly.

The men Braden had planted in the city had pulled her from her wrecked SUV and worked to patch her up. She regained consciousness in a warehouse in Boston, with no recollection on how she got there. Braden promised her Bill's share with conditions. He had asked her to be his arm in the west to which she quickly agreed. *I mean, ten fucking million.*

As the world descended into chaos it was easy for Lilith to double deal, squander her money and run things the way she wanted. It was easy to amass loyal followers. The trick was unrelenting violence. She had aspirations to clean up the city, to properly fortify it and create her own empire in the west with the intentions on taking Braden out herself. She pursed her lips as her thoughts and memories chugged along in her brain. She had anticipated the government would regain some control, but not to the extent that the Federation had managed in the last few years. At first, their efforts were scattered and uncoordinated and attacks often left massive casualties on both sides with little ground changing hands. But now... Now they seem to have a more focused commander and a talented Special Forces team with a direct goal of taking out Braden Murphy. It was only a matter of time before they step up their attacks in Las Vegas.

Lilith paced back and forth wishing she had better spent her money on building her empire but for now, she had to make due and hope that the fight in the east buys her time to shore up her resources and defenses. *Fucking infighting. Damn it Lilith... You're CIA! You should have seen this coming.*

CHAPTER 1

July 29th, 2021

Las Vegas, Nevada

Welcome to Fabulous Las Vegas! Take in a show! Have a romantic dinner! Experience one of dozens of themed casinos! Experience, DEATH. The tattered banner had been spray painted over long ago. Years before One Four Delta had made their way into the city. But the black painted **DEATH** still made Nella Saba shudder as she walked by. It's not that she was afraid of death, at times she even welcomed it. The thought of just laying down her rifle, removing her chest rig and easing into his cold embrace. It was on her mind more often than not these days. More so in the last twenty-four hours.

She reached out her left arm and quietly moved another tattered banner out of her way, her rifle's point of aim straight ahead, as though a target had already presented itself. Lowering the banner quietly behind her, Nella took in a deep breath. The plastic clips on her chest rigged creaked and groaned under the stress put on them by her expanding chest. The sad fact about a world at war is that death becomes common place. People die. Friends die. She had been on the wrong end of death dealing for too long when she was leader of the Rapier Squad, a special operations team for the Republic Sabers in Pittsburgh. Her and her partner Aaron Walsh defected when the Sabers leader, General Khalid Almasi started to lose his grip on things and his violence became uncontrollable.

As she moved quietly through the entrance of the once bustling Miracle Mile Mall her thoughts fell back onto death as though he were an old school friend she had long since parted ways with and they were now headed for a reunion. Thoughts of how their meeting would be. Of whether it would be quick. Of whether it would be painless. Her thoughts were so deep that she barely heard the door off to her right as it creaked open. The hinges all but seized.

Her hand tightened around the pistol grip of her rifle as her heart jumped into her throat. It pounded like a jackhammer on concrete. The thoughts of death forced out of her mind by a rush of blood and the instincts of her training. Her eyes scanned the abandoned, garbage filled hallway landing quickly on an overturned kitchen island moved from a nearby store. *Probably a Pottery Barn*, she thought as she moved. Her boots took her quickly towards her newfound cover as though they had a mind of their own. Blackened blood stains spattered the remaining dusty glass of the store fronts where the remains of their former employees lay decaying in a pile. Taking quiet deep breaths, Nella settled into her position behind the kitchen island. *In through the nose. Out through the mouth. In through the nose. Out through the mouth.* She calmed herself, her heart and her thoughts. The door a few feet in front of her now, pushed further open. Partially obstructed by more debris, the force pushing on the other side of the door groaned in exhaustion as it struggled to make its way to Nella.

"Fucking bullshit mall," screamed a voice behind the door.

"I know man, but she wants the mall swept. Said there's bound to be more of them since there weren't any bodies," another voice chimed in.

The door shuddered. Then, flung open, as a camo-clad man tumbled to the floor from the other side. Nella flipped her rifle off safe. The owner of the second voice, a man dressed in black cargo pants, a grey t-shirt and a tan plate carrier stepped through the now cleared doorway with a wide grin on his face. With a chuckle, he reached out and helped the other man up. The camo-clad man, drenched in sweat from his fight with the door had an AK-47 slung across his back and a second, more familiar rifle in his hands. Nella recognized the black G36-C with a red maple leaf embossed on the magazine housing in an instant. This rifle belonged to Henry Carson.

"Right, let's get this over with eh," said the man in the plate carrier.

"Yeah, fuck this place. I wish we pulled guard duty, but she always has her bitches do it. Must be nice to be Hernandez and Edwards. That blonde... I tell ya..." he paused as a slight movement from Nella caught his attention. "What the fu...." The sounds of two shots from Nella's suppressed M4 rang out through the halls of the Miracle Mile Mall.

Nella waited. Nearly five minutes had passed since her

shots were fired. She listened as though her life depended on it, and as a matter of fact, it did. She hadn't seen the rest of her team for nearly twenty-four hours. They began their incursion into Las Vegas just after dawn and in the first hour they had encountered an ambush. An explosion, possibly a grenade or RPG she couldn't be sure, separated the team and that was the last she had seen of Henry Carson, Brynn Parker and Frank Simmons. In the ensuing firefight she ordered Aaron Walsh and William Heart to fall back as they were overwhelmed with firepower and down half their team. She was further separated from Walsh and Heart after taking a wrong turn through the Aria Resort shopping center. *One Four Delta* as they had come to be known, was no more.

Snapping herself back to the present, Nella slowly pulled herself to her feet. Her black hair, matted with dust and sweat looked like dreadlocks. Her olive drab combat pants, stained with the dark brownish black colour of dried blood. Her ammunition, low. She crept forward with her rifle at the ready and scanned for any signs of movement further down the hall. Her boots crunched chunks of broken glass and tile as she inched closer to the two men. A full minute passed by the time she closed in on the positions of the two most recent men sent to meet Death. Nella paused a moment and stared at her fallen quarry. They looked almost at peace as they lay on the dirty blood-stained marble flooring of the mall. She gathered up Henry's G36-C rifle, some magazines and a single M67 fragmentation grenade from the soldier dressed in black. His name was *Holyfield*, or so his name tag said, Nella noticed a folded piece of paper poking out of the man's shirt pocket. She grabbed the paper and unfolded it, smearing a few fresh blood flecks. It was a list scribbled hastily in pen:

Fed. Soldier = $100 d. / $150 a.

Fed. Officer = $500 d. / $600 a.

Fed. Spec Ops = $1000 d. / $1200 a.

Fed. Spec

The list ended abruptly. Nella stared at the list for a moment, trying to make sense of it. D and A. Is that dead and alive? She thought. She tapped the list with her index finger, before pocketing the list and standing up. She needed to move before someone saw her.

CHAPTER 2

July 29th, 2021

Las Vegas, Nevada

A large lumbering man groaned in exhaustion as he pulled on Aaron Walsh's leg. Sweat ran down his forehead and into his beard, catching the light and sparkling like diamonds. His physique was that of a professional wrestler, large and hulk-like. So large, that his SWAT body armor looked as though it were made for a child. The straps set as loose as they could go, still pressed tight to his body. He pulled Aaron across the street and made his way towards the crumpled Eiffel Tower of the Paris Hotel and Casino. Smoke stained the concrete black around the missing windows of the hotel. The air from the hotel smelled like burning fabric and garbage. The once busy Las Vegas Strip now littered with charred vehicles, bodies and large bits of building.

Gunfire erupted from a nearby side street and jolted Aaron awake. Blinking rapidly, forcing his eyes to focus he tried to figure out where he was. The bright sun pierced his eyes like lasers, causing a slight burning sensation. *I better be fucking* dead, he thought angrily. As his vision slowly returned to normal, all he could see was blue sky mixed with black smoke. A pain shot through his head as he looked around trying to get a bearing on his location. A sort of congested pain, like he had a cold, but it filled his entire head. He tried to remember what had happened. He stared into the hazy blue sky. He remembered moving quietly through a side street to flank a Western Mountain Alliance position with Brynn, but that was about it. There was a faint memory of a trash can toppling over, maybe, he couldn't quite remember. His memory just kind of ended there. He had no idea that a W.M.A. Scout had followed them. He also had no idea that an explosion had knocked him out separating him from his team. The thoughts raced through his head like the *Formula 1* cars he used to watch as a kid. He still had not realized he was moving. Being dragged across the ground by a kitted out lumberjack dragging a recently toppled tree.

His head bumped against some rubble. Snapping back from his thoughts, Aaron finally realized he was moving. Straining his neck to look towards his feet, he finally saw the man dragging him by the Paris Hotel. He quietly reached down to his leg for his pistol. A pain shot down his arm. He fought off a groan as he reached his arm further, finally reaching his holster. Empty. *Where's my fucking gun,* he thought. Another pain shot through his head. He let his arm go limp, no longer able to fight through the pain. He stared into the sky a few moments longer. His arm scraped over something hard. He felt his fingers run across a piece of rebar. *Lucky.*

Aaron's back began to burn as the man relentlessly pulled him across the hot Las Vegas pavement. His t-shirt had bunched up, exposing his bare back. The man finally dropped Aaron's legs and took a moment to rest. They had nearly reached the crumpled Eiffel Tower now and the summer sun seemed to be shining extra bright today, despite the hazy sky. Aaron slowly sat up. Careful to not make a sound. The lumberjack man wiped sweat from his brow with his right forearm. Aaron quietly pulled his right leg in, then his left. The lumberjack man pulled a water bottle from his vests side pouch and began to turn around as he twisted off the cap. Aaron rose to his feet. The bottle cap seemed to slowly fall to the ground as though it were as light as a feather, but it went unnoticed by the SWAT dressed lumberjack who was startled to see Aaron standing there. His trophy, who moments ago was unconscious to the world, was now brandishing a piece of rebar like a samurai sword. The man's hands released the water bottle, leaving it to join the cap on the ground, as they quickly shot towards his M4 rifle slung across his chest. Aaron dove, lashing out with the piece of rebar. The metal bar slammed into the handguard of the rifle, cracking the plastic, stopping the man from raising it. Aaron quickly swung the metal bar upwards striking the man under the chin. Blood sprayed from his mouth as he stumbled backwards over the rubble. Aaron dove in, raising the bar above his head, preparing to strike his captor. The man kicked out, slamming the heel of his boot into Aaron's stomach, forcing him to drop his only weapon and clutch his gut. The blow forced the wind from his lungs. What little food Aaron had in his stomach was now racing to his mouth.

"Stay down," the man groaned through chipped teeth.

Aaron reached for the piece of rebar but a kick to the side of his head stopped him in his tracks. His ear began to ring as the pain radiated through his already pounding skull. Aaron rolled onto his side still clutching his stomach from the previous kick, still reaching for the bar with his right hand. The man stepped closer and placed his heavy black boot on Aaron's gloved hand.

"AHHH!" Aaron screamed. The pain was excruciating. The man put more pressure onto his hand digging his boot into the concrete. Aaron's scream grew louder. Spit flying from his mouth and finding a home in his beard. A burst of machine erupted from a nearby side street, followed by a few muffled pops of semi-automatic fire. The man unslung his rifle and aimed at Aaron's head. He paused. Aaron took a deep breath and closed his eyes.

CRACK! A stray round whizzed by from the nearby firefight. The man, startled, released Aaron's hand from under his boot as he stepped back looking for the source of the round. Aaron sprang to life. He grabbed the piece of rebar and launched himself upwards. He struck the side of the man's head as hard as he could, knocking him down. Without a pause Aaron stepped over his captor and struck him in the head with as much strength as he could muster. He let out a sigh of relief and dropped the bar at his feet. The nearby gunfire had stopped now and a few birds had taken back to the skies. Aaron knelt next to his fallen attacker, his green t-shirt still bunched up under the back of his vest from being dragged along the ground, but he ignored it. He rummaged through the man's vest pockets, removed the magazines, and placed them in his own vest. Unclipping the sling from the M4 rifle he stood up and checked the state of the weapon. The weight told him the magazine was nearly full and he quietly pulled the bolt partially back, slightly exposing a chambered round.

Aaron turned on his heels and made his way past the Paris Hotel and through a side door into the Miracle Mile Mall. The old decaying mall littered with garbage and bodies smelled stale and rotten. The stench lingered in his nostrils, assaulting him with every breath he took. He pushed through a service hallway towards an opening into the main hall. The lack of swinging double doors at the end of the hall caught his attention and he slowed his pace, stepping more deliberately. He thought how someone most likely removed them for firewood. Reaching the large doorway seconds later, he crouched down and took a

breath. He listened. He could hear footsteps in the main courtyard. A small concert stage sat in the center. The lights had
been removed from the overhead scaffolding and replaced with
a make-shift gallows. The footsteps seemed to be fading slightly.
It sounded like a pair of soldiers, maybe more. Aaron took a
deep breath and slowly exhaled. He moved towards the entrance
and slowly peered into the courtyard. Two soldiers walking side-
by-side moved down the corridor away from him. Neither of
them speaking as they stepped over the blackened decaying bodies that littered the floor. Aaron raised his rifle and aimed down
the iron sights. He moved slightly to get a better position behind
a dusty garbage can. As he moved, his boot knocked an empty
soda can and sent it crashing across the marble flooring. The
clanging sound of the can bouncing and rolling on the floor
echoed throughout the empty mall.

The two soldiers spun in place and immediately began to
fire at Aaron. The rounds from their rifles cracked through the
air as they passed by him, slamming into the white and grey tile
walls of the mall. Chips of tile sprayed through the air as Aaron
made a move. He sprinted across the hallway as he returned fire.
His un-aimed shots missed both soldiers and shattered a glass

wall behind them. Aaron slid into cover behind a larger pillar in the center of the hall. The shards of glass slid across the dusty marble flooring as the two soldiers dove for cover amongst the incoming rounds.

"Where's Holyfield and Metcalfe?" screamed one of the soldiers.

Aaron reloaded his rifle letting the empty magazine fall helplessly to the floor as he slammed a full one in and released the bolt catch. He aimed down the iron sights of the M4 rifle he only recently acquired.

"I have no fucking idea!" the other soldier shouted over the renewed sounds of muzzle blast and the cracking of rounds overhead. Aaron ducked back into cover. He was out gunned and running low on ammo. Chunks of drywall from the pillar exploded into the air as rounds tore through it like tissue paper. One of the rounds grazed Aaron's right shoulder, sending a spray of blood out onto the dusty floor.

CHAPTER 3

July 29th, 2021

Las Vegas, Nevada

The two W.M.A. soldiers had Aaron pinned. His pillar of cover slowly dwindling as the bullets ripped and tore chunks of drywall away, exposing the concrete behind it. His world growing slower by the second as time began to slow to a crawl. Aaron reloaded his final magazine into his rifle as he scanned behind him, looking for a way out. His breathing was heavy with exhaustion and his arm covered in blood from his fresh bullet wound as he turned and fired another two shots towards his attackers. One of them let out a scream of pain as Aaron's rounds found their target.

"You good, Carl?" a voice shouted over the gunfire. Aaron could not make out the muffled response from the second soldier. The one he assumes he had just shot.

"Good, then get the fu…"

A loud metallic thud rang out, barely audible to Aaron over the gunfire, but it was a recognizable enough sound. A sound he's heard over years of fighting. A grenade. He took a deep breath, shut his eyes, and braced for the explosion. Hoping the shit life he led would not pass before his eyes, he thought of Nella, Henry and his teammates.

The explosion was deafening. The concussive force shook the remaining glass on the nearby store fronts. Debris zipped by Aaron as he tucked himself behind his nearly decimated pillar, rifle nestled into his lap. His arms wrapped around his legs like a scared child. A few seconds later footsteps crunched their way across the chunks of drywall, ceramic tiles and glass shards that had been sent across the hall. But Aaron couldn't hear anything over the ringing in his ears. Moving carefully, the source of the footsteps crunched their way around Aaron's pillar and revealed a pleased and relieved looking Nella Saba.

"Hey," she said quickly. "Time to go. You good?"

Aaron, still shook and ears still ringing, stared at Nella as though she were speaking an alien language.

"Seriously, you alright… Shit, you're bleeding," she said. The concern in her voice was evident. She made her way back over to the two soldiers and began to search through their gear for bandages or whatever first-aid items she could find.

"I'm fine…" he grumbled, finally as he tried to stand. His legs wobbled as though he were on a boat in stormy seas. Bracing himself on the gutted pillar, Aaron reached for the gauze bandage that Nella pulled from the W.M.A. soldier and started packing the wound in his shoulder. Grunting in pain, he tied off the bandage. "We should keep moving," he said through gritted teeth.

Making their way through the desolate mall, Nella and Aaron kept quiet. Pausing often to listen to their surroundings. Nella led the way down the litter filled hallways. The muzzle of her M4 scanning for targets as she moved. The occasional pops of distant gunfire bounced around the empty mall, slowing Nella and Aaron's movements. Nella paused and pointed to an old Chipotle Mexican Grill. She motioned to Aaron to watch the halls as she pressed in to clear the former restaurant. Letting out a light groan, Aaron adjusted his rifle in his arms and began to scan the surrounding hallways.

Five minutes had passed before Nella returned with a smile on her face. Her rifle slung tight across her chest with the bungee cord sling keeping it in place. Each hand gripped tightly to a tin of beans. She tossed the tin in her right hand to Aaron who winced as he caught it.

"Sorry," Nella whispered. Aaron grumbled in response and followed her further into the derelict restaurant, slowly closing the door behind him, taking extra care not to make noise as he followed her into the kitchen. Still smiling, Nella unzipped the top pocket on her tactical vest and pulled out a heater pack for heating military rations. She quietly pulled an upside-down pot from a nearby rack and after wiping the pot clean, poured some water from her canteen into it and placed the heater into the water. Aaron hacked at both tins of beans with a rusty kitchen knife he fished out of the industrial dishwasher until the lids were twisted and jagged. He peeled the lids back and quietly placed the cans into the rapidly heating water.

"Lukewarm beans are better than cold, right?" Nella asked.

Aaron nodded, then checked over his blood-soaked bandage.

***

Finishing the tin of beans almost immediately had satiated Nella's appetite. She set the empty can down next to her and wiped her face on the back of her gloved hand, trying every-thing in her power to stifle a burp. Staring at Aaron Walsh as he slurped the last remaining bean juice from his tin, she smiled and felt a warmth roll over her, heating her from head to toe. Her unwelcomed thoughts of death faded almost immediately at the sight of her friend. Aaron's bean filled grin quickly snapped her from her daze and she shook her head as if to clear it.

"What the hell happened out there?" Aaron asked.

"Holy shit! Right?" Nella responded a little too enthusias-tically. "I remember following Henry down an alley by the old New York New York when all that gunfire broke out. I lost sight of him after that RPG kicked up dust. I ended up taking cover through an open door," she took a deep breath. "Once I looked out, everyone was gone, and the shots were moving away. Did you see anything?"

Aaron sat, motionless. After a few seconds that felt like

an hour he started to shake his head back and forth. His face began to flush, and his dirt covered cheeks shone bright red. He cleared his throat.

"I… I uh… I got knocked out by the blast," he said sheepishly. "Came to and nothing. No Henry, no Brynn… No you. Just some big fucker dragging me across the hot ass ground like a twelve-point buck. Prick didn't even have the decency to put me out of my misery." Aaron pulled his canteen from vest pouch and took a large swig, ignoring the water streaming from the corners of his mouth and into his beard.

Nella stared for a moment gathering her thoughts, but mostly letting Aaron have some time to compose himself. She was reaching for her own canteen when she remembered the list she found on of the soldiers in the mall. Fishing it from her vest, she passed it to Aaron who hesitantly reached out and took it.

"I wonder if it has something to do with this?" she asked in a tone that wasn't much of a question. "I think they are collecting bounties on us. That's why he didn't kill you.

"Where'd you get this?" Aaron asked.

"Pulled it off a guy before I met up with you. He had Henry's rifle too," she said motioning to the G36-C with the red

Maple Leaf on the magazine resting quietly against the wall next to her.

"He's alive…" Aaron said quietly to reassure her.

"Yeah, I'm sure of…"

The crash at the front of the restaurant shot a hole through her thoughts. Before either of them could grab their weapons and move they were staring at the suppressed barrel of a rifle.

CHAPTER 4

July 29th, 2021

Las Vegas, Nevada

Out of breath and out gunned, Frank Simmons slung his M14 rifle across his back and hauled himself up into a broken window of the New York New York hotel and casino. Landing with a hard thud, dust kicked up all around him, clouding his vision. Frank pulled himself to his feet and began to scan the vast and dark emptiness of the former bustling casino. The slot machines, untouched for years now, had a thick deposit of dust covering them. Light pierced through broken windows and holes in the walls, illuminating the gaming floor just enough for Frank to move his way inward. Unslinging his rifle, he cautiously scanned his surroundings as he moved. His footing was deliberate, trying not to make noise has he glided almost ghost like across the debris strewn floor. *What the fuck happened?* he thought to himself as he swung around to scan the way he had come. Satisfied no one had followed him in through the window, Frank continued his push further into the darkness of the New York New York.

Racking his brain as he moved, he couldn't quite figure out what happened. Everything had been going according to plan. They had successfully snuck into the city and made their way to the strip undetected. They had almost successfully reached their rendezvous point at the New York New York when Frank decided to push further up and suggest to Henry that he try to gain some higher ground. He had just pushed passed Brynn Parker and William Heart when the deafening boom of an RPG had rung out and he dove for cover into an offshoot of the alley.

He froze in place when he remembered seeing the smoke from the explosive engulf Aaron Walsh. *Fuck*…Standing still for what felt like an eternity, Frank was jerked back to the present by the sound of rocky rubble crumbling from a nearby hallway. Flushing all thoughts of the last day from his head, Frank quickly and carefully moved forward towards an overturned poker table and quietly rested the barrel of his M14 on it. Peering through his sight with his right eye, he scanned for the source of the noise.

"… Hear they got the big guy?" a voice said.

"Sure did," a second voice responded. "Got one of the women too." Two soldiers rounded the corner from a nearby hallway and made their way towards Frank's position as they chatted. One of the soldiers carrying an RPG slung over his shoulder was a wider set man of average height. The other with a rifle, was tall and skinny.

"Pretty sure I got a couple with the beast here," the RPG soldier said with a light chuckle to his voice.

"You know, we get more if we capture 'em, or bring back a body," the rifleman said, slightly annoyed. "Ya can't go turning 'em into a mist all the time…"

Quietly as he could, Frank flipped his rifles safety off. The two soldiers were fifteen meters or so away. He took a deep breath. Feeling the trigger on the tip of his index finger, he exhaled and squeezed. The report of the suppressed M14 was loud enough to echo off every surface in the dark casino. The

RPG soldier hit the ground before the rifleman could finish his conversation. Frank shifted and rapidly followed his first shot with a second, the 7.62mm round finding a home in the rifleman's left shoulder.

Screaming in pain, the rifleman dove for cover behind a nearby stack of slot machines and returned fire. The rounds from his uncontrolled burst slammed into the poker table protecting Frank as dust launched into the air. Frank adjusted his position to the left of the overturned table and fired three shots towards the slot machine stack sending glass, metal and electronics soaring into the air. Shuffling on the other side of the stack caught Franks attention. He shifted his aim to the right. He fired. The single round punched through the soldier's throat as he stepped out from behind cover to fire. His finger squeezed the trigger as he fell, sending a surge of rounds flying over Frank's shoulder and into the ceiling. Flat out on his back, the tall skinny rifleman attempted to move back behind the slot machines, but it was hopeless. His grip relaxed on the rifle and his other hand that was clutching his throat flopped to the carpeted floor.

Frank continued to scan the area for a moment before approaching the W.M.A. soldiers. Searching their pockets, he found nothing worth taking except a tattered and now blood-soaked notepad. He quickly flipped through the notepad filled with nothing but crude doodles, stick figure pornography and portrait style drawing of a woman done in pen. As Frank tried shove the notepad into his pant leg pocket, a small slip of paper, no bigger than a standard post-it note fell from the back of the notepad. A short list on the paper read:

Fed. Soldier = $100 d. / $150 a.

Fed. Officer = $500 d. / $600 a.

Fed. Spec Ops = $1000 d. / $1200 a. - 2 female, 4 male - ambush

Fed. Spec Ops Cmdr. = $3000 a.

Frank stared at the list for a moment taking it all in. His eyes hung up on the hastily scribbled 2 female, 4 male – ambush. His thoughts began to race, and his hands began tremble. Had they not been successful in entering the city? How long had they been watched before they were ambushed? Did these soldiers kill or capture everyone else? Panic was just starting to set in when a muffled nearby explosion brought him back. Stuffing the note into his pocket, Frank Simmons picked up his rifle and headed towards source of the explosion.

Moving slowly, Frank scanned his surroundings as though he were a meerkat keeping watch for a predator. The vehicles that lined the street were burnt out and had long since been stripped for parts. Frank's eyes wandered to the skeletal remains of tourists that littered the streets as his ears caught the sounds of crows and other birds sounding out overhead. The all-too-quiet nature of the Strip had Frank's heart pounding so hard it was as though it were attempting to burst through his chest. An engine roared to life nearby causing Frank to dive for cover. A second engine spoke up, then a third. Frank crawled into a burnt-out sedan outside of the South entrance to the Miracle Mile Mall and watched as three Humvees raced out of the Bellagio parking garage and take off to the North. They passed two tanks that stood guard at the Bellagio entrance. The well-used Humvee's, each with a soldier manning a machine gun, rolled out of view as they travelled away from Frank and towards the Stratosphere Tower at the other end of the strip. He slowly exited the burnt out sedan taking care not to bang his rifle on the rusty black metal frame.

Frank spun in place, taking a knee, as a short surge of gun-fire echoed out from the mall. He scanned the entrance through his rifle sight. His heart pounding. His hands shaking. The gunfire was silenced by a muffled explosion that cleared the skies of birds. Frank took a deep breath. He continued to scan the entrance. His trigger finger ready to squeeze. Frank was expecting the doors to the mall to burst open and a flood of W.M.A soldiers to flow out ending his life in the shortest gunfight he would ever have been in. But nothing happened. Sighing a deep sigh of relief, Frank reached for the talk button of his Personal Report Radio on his shoulder.

"Carson. It's Frank. You copy?" he whispered into the microphone. Silence. "Saba, Parker, anyone read me?" he whispered again, this time a little louder with more of a waver in his voice. More silence. He looked around for any signs of movement before trying to adjust the volume on his radio. *Maybe it's turned down.* He slid his fingers on his left hand over the radio, until his index finger reached space where the volume dial should be. He yanked the radio down towards his chest and his eyes glared at the bullet hole that tore through the radio.

"Mother fucker," he said louder than he should have. Confident that no one was around, Frank rose to his feet and began to move towards the doors of the mall when a faded sign for a Chipotle Mexican Grill caught his eyes. His stomach panged at the thought of food, a feeling he had been suppressing for the better part of a day. He slowly opened the doors to the mall, noticing that the layer of dust inside had recently been disturbed. Shouldering his rifle, he pressed further into the dilapidated hallways towards a hopeful source of food.

Quietly Frank pulled the front entrance to Chipotle open and scanned the dining area. The large open dining room, littered with overturned tables, chairs and tattered tablecloths. He took note of the obvious signs of recent movement and slowly stepped further into the restaurant. The clang of a pot rang out from the kitchen and Frank snapped his rifle sight to the double doors. His adrenaline kicked into overdrive as he quietly side stepped towards the door in a slight flanking maneuver. He reached the door in a matter of moments and could hear the soft sound of two voices in hushed conversation coming from the kitchen. Reaching for the door with his left hand, rifle at the ready, his foot pulled on a shredded tablecloth pulling a dusty glass beer pitcher to the floor. The crash of the shattering glass rang out through the restaurant. Without hesitation and with the energy of a fired cannonball, Frank burst through the door and his rifle barrel came face to face with Nella Saba and Aaron Walsh staring back at him, stunned and frozen in place.

CHAPTER 5

July 29th, 2021

Las Vegas, Nevada

A dimly lit room filled with dripping pipes sat positioned in the basement of the Bellagio Hotel and Casino. It was a sprawling room that trailed off as far as the eye could see. Unfortunately for Brynn Parker, the blindfold over her eyes kept her from knowing just how far. The whirring of exhaust fans hummed insistently in the room. Brynn, strapped to an old rolling chair placed near the entrance to the maintenance room, licked her dry lips. She bobbed her head as she began to regain consciousness. Her blonde hair, matted with dirt and dried blood moved stiffly as she raised her head. A light groan escaped her lungs, passing over her dry lips and stinging the large cut that ran across her up-per lip and snaked upwards by her left eye. Her arms, bound to the chair with black zap straps were bloody and bruised and the ring finger on her left hand was missing. A blood-soaked ban-daged stub was left in its place. The chair creaked and groaned as Brynn began to struggle against her bindings. *Where the fuck am I?* she thought. The humming of the fans were growing more annoying, grating on her ears like nails on a chalkboard. "Ugh… What happened?" she groaned out loud. Her legs, bound to-gether with zap straps, felt surprisingly okay. She slid her feet forward and the chair rolled slightly. She slid her feet forward again, moving farther this time. The chair rolled another foot along the cement floor. She had no idea where she was or where she was going, she just knew she had to move. No one spoke up, yelled or tried to stop her as she moved. The beat of her heart strengthened as her hopes of escape grew. Her third attempt to roll the chair took her another foot forward. And then, the chair began to roll on its own. It picked up speed as she had unknow-ingly rolled onto a wheelchair ramp.

She slammed into a closed door at the end of the ramp, her knees taking the brunt of the collision. A loud and hollow metallic clang echoed around the seemingly empty room. She winced as the pain shot up and down her legs. Frustrated, she tried to feel along the wall she had just crashed into for a way out of her large prison cell. Her frustrations quickly turned to fear when she heard laughing come from behind her. The hairs on the back of her neck shot up, like tiny soldiers standing at attention.

"I told you not to use the wheely chair," a woman said. Her voice was deep and curt.

"What, I thought it would be funny to give her some hope," another woman said in a more playful tone. Footsteps thudded along the floor as one of the women approached Brynn and spun her chair around. The woman wheeled her back up the ramp and returned her to the spot she had started in, spinning the chair a couple of times. She grabbed the arm rest, jolting pain through Brynn's wounded hand, and leaned in towards her. "…And, it *was* fucking funny," she let out a laugh not unlike a witch's cackle and removed Brynn's blindfold.

The room was dark, but Brynn's eyes had no trouble adjusting. She blinked a few times and focused on the two women standing in front of her. The woman to her right was muscular with a shaved head. Her tanned complexion and large biceps re-flected the few lights that remained on in the room. Brynn bare-ly noticed that the woman was wearing her plate carrier, which barely fit over her large frame, and had her MP5 slung over her shoulder. Her gaze turned to the second woman who was now standing back upright. Her short purple hair stood out against the plain tan overalls she was wearing. Brynn's eyes swept her over. Moving from the shit-eating-grin on the woman's face to the leg holster housing a Colt 1911 pistol on her left leg. The three women stared at each other for nearly a full minute taking each other in when the radio on Brynn's plate-carrier sprang to life with static. The muscular woman calmly reached up and turned the power switch to off. "Looks like one of your friends is still alive," she said. "Unless Holyfield set another trap for them," she added.

Brynn's thoughts began to race. Suddenly she was no lon-ger in a dark maintenance room. She was back on the strip as One Four Delta pushed deeper into their recon of Las Vegas. She remembered taking cover as some Humvee's sped by and after a five-minute listening halt they carried on to the New York New York. She then thought she saw some movement from a balcony above them as they moved down an alley. Convincing herself it was birds she returned to scanning as Frank Simmons pushed by her. That was when a large explosion knocked her backwards, shrapnel tearing her finger off and scarring her face. Her memories were faded from there. She remembered gunfire and being carried a bit, but not much else. The purple haired woman leaned in and flicked Brynn in the center of the forehead, snapping her back to the present.

"Hey, still with us, bitch?" she asked with a twisted smile on her face.

"When's Holyfield getting here?" the muscular woman asked. "I'm fucking sick of guard duty." She was visibly annoyed with having to stand in this dark and damp room when there were more pressing things to attend to.

The door at the end of the ramp dinged as it opened revealing an elevator car. A dark-blonde haired woman with pale skin marched up towards Brynn and the guards who straightened up immediately. The woman was average in height and build. She was dressed almost exactly like Brynn. She had a navy blue, long sleeve shirt on that was partially hidden by a tan plate carrier with a desert camouflage pattern and was wearing olive green pants and a pair of brown hiking boots. She looked like every CIA Agent in every spy movie that Brynn had seen before the world turned to shit. A green bodied shotgun with a telescoping stock and black ridged pump slide sat snug against her back. She was flanked by another two guards, both short but muscular men in tan overalls sporting AK-47's. She approached Brynn, stopping at the top of the ramp only a few feet from her chair. She paused and stared at Brynn. A moment that felt like a day went by before she popped open the clip on the fragmentation grenade pouch of her plate carrier. Brynn's heart leapt as she thought the worst. The woman pulled out a package of cigarettes and removed a single cigarette from the crushed looking package. She lit it with a black Bic lighter that was clipped to her vest by paracord and a carabiner. She let the lighter fall to the end of its cord and took a long haul before lowering it and blowing the smoke towards Brynn.

"Where are your friends?" she asked politely. Her voice was soft and calm. Moving forward towards Brynn so the flickering lights illuminated her face. Brynn could see that her makeup was near perfect. It was almost as though she had once been the star of a Las Vegas show and had never stopped performing despite the war. Brynn gulped back some saliva mixed with blood from the gouge on her face.

"You poor thing," she said sounding worried. She leaned in closer to Brynn and placed a soft hand against her face near her wound. The plastic furniture of the shotgun creaked and groaned as she moved. "Sofia, fetch the first aid kit." The muscular woman unenthusiastically turned and headed down the ramp towards the elevator and out of the room. "We'll get that taken care of, Parker, is it? Yes, Parker, we'll get you cleaned up at once. But… I do need you to tell me where your friends are first. Okay?" Brynn shifted in her chair. The calm tone in the woman's voice added an air of tension that sent a shiver down Brynn's spine.

"I couldn't get anything out of her," the purple haired woman chimed in.

"Of course, you couldn't Sheena. This one's tough. She's going to need more than threats and torture. Go get the man, Heart I think his name is." Brynn's eyes widened at the mention of William Heart's name. "Yeah, I thought that might get me somewhere," the woman said.

"Commander Holyfield!" Sofia Hernandez shouted as she

returned with the first aid kit. "You're needed back up in the Penthouse. There's uh… there's a situation." Sofia's muscles glistened with sweat. It was evident to Brynn that this woman had just hustled her ass off to get back here.

"Watch this one. And radio me once her little friend has been brought down here," Commander Holyfield said, her tone still calm. She flicked her cigarette and left with her two male guards in tow. Sofia dropped the first aid kit on the floor at Brynn's feet, smiled sarcastically and walked back over to the desk against the wall where she began to look through more of Brynn's gear that laid spread out on the stainless steel desktop.

CHAPTER 6

July 29th, 2021

Las Vegas, Nevada

Slurping back the last of the beans that Nella had slightly heated up for him, Frank Simmons wiped his mouth and removed the busted Personal Report Radio from his shoulder. He glanced over it quickly before tossing it to Aaron.

"Got a little lucky…" Simmons said through a pinto bean flavoured burp.

"I'll say," Aaron replied. His fingers tracing around the bullet hole in the radio body. "Mine's gone too. Think I lost it in the ambush."

"Yours working Nells?" Nella, now keeping watch at the

kitchen doors with her M4 gripped tightly in her hands, shook her head back and forth slowly. Simmons stood up, stretching out his lower back and moved over next to Nella. He glanced quickly through the window in the kitchen door before removing her radio from her vest. Leaning against the dusty stainless-steel sink, he plugged the radio into his headset and began to fiddle with the switches. He paused for a moment, then pressed the talk switch. "Carson, you copy?" he said with bated breath. The radio stayed silent. "Any call sign One Four Delta, come in," he said less enthusiastically. More silence. Simmons pulled his headset off in frustration and let it hang down to the floor. "Maybe it's just the batteries. Anyone have any?" he thought out loud. Both Nella and Aaron shook their heads.

Aaron climbed to his feet. Grimacing from the pain shooting down his arm from the bullet wound in his shoulder as he made his way to the kitchen door to relieve Nella of watch. He peered through the small window in the door, scanning for movement. His fire-red beard matted with dust and yet still glistening with sweat. He seemed deep in thought as he scanned the front entrance to the restaurant for movement. The sound of a desk drawer slamming to his left startled him from his daze.

"Find anything useful?" he grumbled to Frank who was exiting a nearby office. Frank just shook his head. Walsh turned his gaze back to the window. "What the fuck even happened out there?" he said after a few moments. No one answered. Nella was checking her map and Simmons was continuing his search for batteries. "I mean, it's like they knew we were coming, like they were hunting us," he said, sounding irritated.

"I… I think they were," Simmons chimed in. He dug around in his pocket and fished out the note he found earlier on the soldiers in the New York New York. "Look," he said showing the note to Nella and Aaron. "See, right here. Lists of rewards for Fed soldiers dead or alive. But right here it says Fed. Spec Ops = $1000 d. / $1200 a. - 2 female, 4 male – ambush."

"Fuckers must've been watching us," Nella said, clenching her fists. "I bet they lured us into that alley. Remember that turn we had to make?"

"I don't remember shit," Aaron said, gruffly, rubbing his head.

"I heard the soldiers I found this on talking," Simmons said, his voice tone lowered. "They said they caught the big guy and one of the women and something about turning one to mist.

I think they caught Brynn."

"What about mist?" Aaron asked.

"You don't think they killed William or Henry, do you?" Nella asked, her voice trembling.

"Not Henry, no…" Simmons said, trailing off.

A noise outside the restaurant startled all three of them. Simmons tossed his radio onto his gear and grabbed Henry's G36-C that was perched against the wall. He quickly and quietly press checked the chamber and moved towards the kitchen door next to Aaron. Nella crouched down next to the sink, her M4 at the ready. Aaron, peering through the window, held up one finger on his left hand. Simmons nodded and slowly pushed the door open. Aaron moved through, followed by Nella, then Simmons. A lone soldier was attempting to pry the door open to a derelict restaurant across the hall. The three fanned out across the dining area. Simmons took a knee behind an over-turned table and attempted to line up a shot on the soldier, but the dirty windows made it difficult to see clearly. Aaron and Nella flanked each side to the entrance doors. Nella raised her rifle. The soldier in the hall turned and moved towards them. Nella flicked her safety off. The soldier moved closer, staggering slightly. Nella's trigger finger tensed, ready to fire a round. The soldier approached the door.

"Fucking hold fire!" Simmons shouted and burst to his feet. He rushed to the door as fast as an Olympic sprinter pushing of their starting blocks. Aaron and Nella barely had time to register what was happening by the time Simmons had burst through the doors and grabbed a hold of the bloody, bruised and dehydrated soldier. A feeling of relief washed over them as he helped Henry Carson into the restaurant.

CHAPTER 7

July 29th, 2021

Las Vegas, Nevada

Henry sat in the office chair gulping down water faster than he ever had before in his life. The streams of water pouring down his face washed the dirt away and dripped onto his blood-soaked plate carrier. The water that did make it into his mouth felt like what he could only imagine heaven felt like. Nella handed him the last tin of pinto beans she could find and had just finished heating with the squad's last heater pack. Henry grabbed it from her as though he had never seen food before in his life. Coughing and choking only a few times, Henry polished off the beans in a matter of moments. He took a deep breath and smiled at his team. Lukewarm beans dotted his plate carrier. He flicked them off and contorted in pain as he attempted to pull the plate carrier up over his head. Simmons helped pull it off him as blood trickled from Henry's side. Henry grimaced again and grabbed at his wound to put pressure on it. The gauze he had stuffed under his vest in a vain attempt to stem the bleeding was soaked through with blood. Frank pulled an Israeli Bandage from his pack and began to wrap it tight around Henry's abdomen.

"Where's Brynn and William?" Henry asked through gritted teeth. No answer. Aaron shifted on his feet, maintaining watch through the door. "Hey, is that my rifle?" Henry said, excitedly pointing to his G36-C leaning peacefully against the wall.

"Yeah!" Nella said, peering from the storage room off the far wall of the kitchen. "I found it on two guys patrolling the other side of the mall. Some dude named Holyfield had it."

"Holyfield… Why does that name sound familiar?" Simmons asked, tightening the bandage around Henry's midsection. Henry flinched.

Standing up with a slight wobble, Henry straightened his

bunched up tan t-shirt and hobbled over to his rifle. Picking it up, he felt a near instant feeling of relief. Like seeing an old friend after several years apart. He removed the magazine and ejected the round from the chamber. The action felt smooth in his hands. After placing the ejected round back into the magazine, he seated the rounds by tapping the magazine on his left thigh. A jolt of pain shot through his body from the wound on his side. He slid the magazine back into the rifle until it clicked, locking into place. He gave the magazine two hard wraps on the bottom to ensure it was in place. He turned back towards Frank Simmons, who was packing the first aid kit into in his bag. Henry twisted his lips in thought. Remembering back to their briefing before they left for Las Vegas. The Commander of Special Operations Force Recon, Colonel Howard, whom Henry had the pleasure of serving under in Afghanistan in 2008 had talked at length about the brutality of the small Western Mountain Alliance force in Vegas and their new Commander. Pausing for a moment, he finally answered Frank. "The Commander of the W.M.A. is a Lilith Holyfield. I wonder if there's a relation?"

"Maybe," Nella chimed in. "But how did he end up with your rifle?"

"During that ambush, I had to rush forward for cover. I tucked in behind an old Humvee and turned just in time to see you falling back down the alley when a second RPG went off. I took some shrapnel, I think…" Henry paused, pressing on his wound before continuing. "… I tried to run towards the New York, when a group of guys opened fire on me. I fired back but my weapon jammed, so I just ran. Hard." Henry took a long, deep breath and licked his lips which had been dry since they landed in Nevada. "I leapt over a barricade," he continued, "but the rifle barrel snagged. They had me under effective fire, so I cut my sling and fucked off. I managed to make it to the Excalibur and must have passed out. Woke up a little delirious and tried to make my way back to our vehicles but I had to take cover from a patrol and ended up back here." Henry sat back down in the office chair. His rifle laying across his lap. His side, shooting with pain.

Aaron waved Frank over to relieve him of watch. He quietly slumped down against the wall next to Henry and picked at some remaining bean stuck in his teeth, ignoring the pain radiating from the bullet wound in his shoulder. He continued to alternate between picking his teeth and his beard for a few moments before finally breaking the uncomfortable silence in the room. "So, what's the plan?" he said bluntly. No response. He looked around the room at each remaining member of One Four Delta. Henry Carson stared blankly at his rifle. Frank Simmons stared intently out the kitchen door window. Nella Saba stared daggers back at him. He guessed she knew what he was going to say, but he had to say it anyway. "'Coz I think we should pull back and regroup with Howard at the F.O.B.".

"Fuck that!" Nella jumped in without any hesitation. "We need to keep going!"

"Keep going? We're fucked! You and Frank are the only ones fit as a fiddle," Aaron said, rising to his feet. He moved closer to Nella, so they were nearly face to face. "In case you forgot, Henry's a little busted up and I've got a bullet in me."

"We can't leave. We can't! Not if William and Brynn are out there. Who knows what this Holyfield will do to them if we don't find them," Nella shouted, her tone reeking of desperation. Henry continued to stare at his rifle. His lips pursed as he thought. Simmons motioned quietly for them to quiet down. "Carson, tell him we're continuing on mission. We need to recon the W.M.A Headquarters. We… We need to find Brynn and William," she said, focusing all her efforts on pleading with Henry.

Henry took a deep breath. His head bobbing up and down in a slow nod before looking up at Aaron, then to Nella. Reading the looks of exhaustion on their faces, Henry nodded faster. His mind made up. "No," he said, "Aaron's right. We need to fall back and regroup. We aren't rescuing anyone in this condition." And without working comms, we've got no back up from Colonel Howard, he thought to himself.

CHAPTER 8

July 29th, 2021

Las Vegas, Nevada

"What do you mean he's dead?" Commander Holyfield asked through gritted teeth. Her hands balled up as her knuckles pressed the desk, determined to punch through the wood. Her shotgun lay across the desktop in front of her. She stared straight ahead. Her green eyes piercing through the two men standing nervously in front of her like lasers. One of the men shifted slightly, the plastic clips on his knee pads creaking as he moved. His hunting camo t-shirt and tan cargo pants were stained with blood. He cleared his throat but didn't speak. "What. Do. You. Mean. He's. Fucking. Dead," she said again. The anger in her voice was terrifying. She straightened up grabbing her shotgun as she moved.

Nervously, the man in camo stepped forward one pace, cleared his throat again and began to speak. "Well, uh Mam. We was... we was searching for the other's like ordered. You know after we ambushed them," he fumbled for his words. "And well, he uh... he was ambushed himself," he paused. Tension in the air grew as he looked around at the guards flanking his Commander.

"Go on," she said.

"We were clearing the area around the mall, right, 'an he took Simpson with him. I was with Marco. We found the red bearded guy. Marco said he was taking him into the Paris rendez-vous point 'an I headed to the mall."

One of the flanking bodyguards asked him where Marco was now. Holyfield didn't move.

"He's uh... he's dead too." The man's eyes darted between the guards and Commander Holyfield as his body began to vibrate nervously. "It was fucked up Mam, it was so quiet then I heard all the gunfire," the soldier swallowed the large wad of spit that had formed in his throat, "...then an explosion. By the time

I got to the mall it was over. They fuckin' got Lopez and Mackey with a grenade. Marco, Simpson and… and your son…"

The blast from the shotgun rang out through the Penthouse, rattling its windows, as Commander Holyfield fired a three-inch, twelve-gauge slug, into the face of the trembling soldier. The soldier standing next to him flinched. His face scrunched up in fear and splattered in a spray of fresh blood. The two male guards both grasped their ears at the sound of the shot. Holyfield pumped the action on the shotgun, ejecting the shell onto the marble floor. The sound of the hollow plastic tube bouncing on the stone echoed around the otherwise quiet room.

***

Outside of Commander Holyfield's office, the man that she didn't shoot, wiped the blood from his face with the front of his shirt. His hands trembled. They hadn't trembled this much since his first tour in Iraq. *That would have been, Jesus, seventeen years ago*, he thought as he stared at his hands. He had friends killed before, lots of them in fact. You don't fight a war and not lose at least a couple. But this time felt different to him. *Don't shoot the messenger my ass.*

He was waiting for the elevator when the two bodyguards pushed open the office door dragging the bloody, faceless body of the camo wearing man. The elevator dinged and the doors opened. Stepping aside, he let the two men drag his former friend into the small square box, the white tile smeared with blood. "Thanks, Dunk," one of the guards said, "and listen, find those fucks, or you know," he pointed down at the body.

By the time the elevator returned, the smeared blood had been mostly cleaned up. The grout was stained and will likely stay that way until the building is destroyed. Dunk stepped into the elevator and pressed the button for the maintenance levels. His hands still trembling. No one ever called him by his real name of James Turner. Especially since his resemblance to the actor Michael Clarke Duncan was almost uncanny. On the elevator ride down, Dunk thought about that first tour in Iraq. He had been fresh out of boot and assigned the M249 Squad Automatic Weapon. The SAW most people called it. His large stature made the gun look small in his hands and it made wielding it easy. The first time he lost a friend was when they were clearing an alleyway in Fallujah the first month he was there. He had just emptied a two-hundred round box from his SAW down the alleyway to suppress the enemy and ducked back into cover to reload. His squad mate Ricky, a skinny white boy straight out of a Tennessee trailer park, who Dunk had gotten to know quite well over the month, stepped into the alley to lay down a deliberate rate of fire when a sniper round thumped into his chest. Ricky dropped to the ground, wheezing in pain and clutching at his chest. The plate in his plate carrier had managed to stop the bullet. *At worst he's looking at a couple broken ribs*, Dunk thought. Grabbing the left shoulder strap of Ricky's chest rig, Dunk started to pull him into cover, but it was too late. The sniper's follow-up shot was per-fect and found its home in Ricky's T-box, the space on a person's head between their eyes and down to their upper lip. Ricky went limp and Dunk froze. His hands trembled like they are now in the elevator all these years later. *It's Ricky all over again*, Dunk thought. The elevator dinged, snapping him back to reality. The doors opened and he made his way towards Sofia Hernandez and Sheena Edwards who were still guarding Brynn. "I need to have a little chat with her. Boss wants you back up top," he said.

Brynn Parker was dehydrated, bloodied and bruised but that didn't stop her from staring daggers at Sheena and Sofia as they walked away leaving her with this man, Dunk they had called him. She continued to stare at them until the elevator doors closed and then darted her eyes to Dunk, who was tidying up the used medical supplies on the table. His back was to her, but she didn't try to move or escape. Instead, she studied him, sized him up. She took note of his large size, his Arnold Schwarzenegger like biceps and his shaved head. He was wearing a desert camouflage t-shirt and cargo pants that were either the same pattern or slightly different, but it was too dark for her to tell. His combat boots were worn well, she could see how the brown leather had stretched and given way over time. He had a pistol holster on his left leg with a black pistol, probably a Colt 1911, it's always a 1911, she thought. He wasn't wearing a chest rig or plate carrier, but since she assumed this was their HQ, that didn't strike her as odd. What really stuck out to her was the way his hands trembled while he cleaned the table top.

"Name's Dunk," he said. Brynn didn't respond. "Well, actually, it's James Turner but everyone calls me Dunk." He dusted his hands and turned around to face Brynn. The table let out an audible groan as he leaned his hulking weight against it. He paused for a moment, staring at her unblinking, battered and

scared face. "Worked you over good did they? Those bitches.
Never liked 'em much," he said folding his arms across his chest.
His voice was deep and full of bass. Brynn continued to stare
at Dunk. He could tell she was trying to work out his reason
for being there. Dunk took in a slow deep breath through his
nose and let it out just as slow through his mouth. "Well," he
said. "Shit's pretty well fucked up in here now. I mean, it had
been for a while. Holyfield began to slip after the NBF fell out
east and the Fed's moved this way. Hole up in a fuckin' desert,
reeaaal smart." Dunk rolled his eyes and gave another pause.
Brynn continued to stare, blinking every few moments to keep
her eyes moist. Unfolding his arms, Dunk pushed himself up
onto the table and adjusted the pistol holster on his leg. "Anyway, supplies and morale here are low. Holyfield thought her
ambush yesterday would be a big win for her. You know, show
her strength or whatever, but we captured two of you and the
rest bounced. That is after they took out around twenty of us…
including Holyfield's son."

Brynn's eyes finally moved away from Dunk. She looked
around the room quickly. There was no one else there. She
couldn't hear anything either, other than a wheeze in her breath

and the table groaning under Dunk's weight. "Why are you telling me this?" she asked.

"I want out," Dunk said matter-of-factly.

"Out? Out of here?"

"Yes. Out of this shit-hole of a city. Out of this shit-hole
of an operation. I've got good intel and I figure the Fed's could
use it."

"You said you caught two and the rest bounced?" she
asked, trying to piece together a plan.

"Yep. You and some guy named Heart. He's up with
Holyfield now so I can't risk talking to him, but you're close to
the old maintenance access so it should be an easy exfil. The rest
of your squad were last seen around the Miracle Mile Mall, but
that was a while ago now."

Brynn asked if he was sure the others left and he told her
he was sure as shit. She had relaxed a bit now but was still wary
of this 'Dunk' man who had stood up from the table and was
now moving around behind her. She heard the flick of a knife
and her body tensed. He grabbed her wrists. "I'll help you outta
here and you help me secure a place with the Feds, hoorah?" he
said.

"Marines?" she asked.

"3rd Battalion, 1st Marines. Did three tours in Iraq and one in Afghanistan. Was gunning to be a Master Sergeant till a Talib IED took my right leg." He knocked at his leg with the knife and a faint metallic ping sounded out from under his pants. Brynn took a breath and nodded. Dunk slipped the blade of his knife between her wrists and cut the zip-ties.

CHAPTER 9

July 29th, 2021

Federation Staging Area

Area 51, Nevada

The tan pick-up truck was still parked on the hill of the Gass Peak trailhead where they had left it two days ago. It was relatively well hidden amongst the arid landscape and reconnaissance showed that WMA patrols never ventured this way but Henry Carson still worried about leaving it unattended. Limping over to the passenger side door, Henry called out shotgun as he got in. Frank Simmons rolled his eyes and made his way to the driver's side and threw open the door. With William Heart gone, Simmons was the team's backup driver. He had the experience and liked to think of himself as a professional driver and he probably could have been if he hadn't joined the army. Nella and Aaron grabbed a few bottles of water from the truck bed and climbed into the back seats. Once the doors were shut, Simmons fired up the engine and sped off towards Area 51. Dust and rocks kicked up behind the rear tires as they slipped on the loose ground. After a few moments of bumpy cross country terrain, the truck turned onto an old overgrown ATV trail and the ride was a bit smoother, much to the relief of everyone in the truck. Henry opened the bottle of water passed to him over his shoulder by Nella and took a long and much needed sip. A refreshed *ahhhh* escaped his throat. He capped the bottle and reached for the radio handset. After a quick pause and a breath, he keyed the handset's button.

"One this is One Four Delta, SITREP, over." The radio spouted static.

"One, One Four Delta, SITREP, OVER," Henry said again, louder this time. More static.

"Piece of shit," Simmons said, smacking the dashboard.

"One, One Four Delta, SITREP, OVER."

"One send," the radio sprang to life. Simmons smiled as

though he solved the world's problems.

"One Four Delta… Enemy: Unknown number of combatants in Las Vegas proper, ten to twenty KIA," Henry paused and took a breath. "Friendly: two MIA and two wounded," he paused again. "We were ambushed inside the city and were separated. Four of us managed to regroup and are now en route to rearm and redeploy, over." Henry released the handset key and took another swig of water.

"One, roger, debrief when you're back, out." The radio crackled and then went silent. Henry replaced the handset to its holder and took another gulp of water. The occupants of the truck were silent which made the sounds of brush scrapping the doors seem as loud as a gun range.

***

Five hours had passed since they left Gass Peak and Simmons finally made the turn onto the road to Area 51. The truck slowed to a crawl as an M1A1 Abrams tank that guarded the main gate took aim at them. This part always made Henry and the rest of the team nervous. One exhausted tanker and they would all be the new owners of property in whatever after-life they believed in. Luckily, today wasn't that day. The truck slowed to a stop at the gate and the tank's barrel returned to scanning the horizon. The guard took his time walking down from the tower, a fairly new private that either pulled the short straw or fucked up bad enough to get gate duty. Simmons put the driver's window down and Nella shoved Aaron awake who snorted loudly as he sat up. Henry could see the guard clearly now. He was a young guy, about twenty or so, clean shaven and clearly hasn't seen much action as his uniform is still pristine. He was nervous as he approached the truck, his right hand gripping the pistol grip of his M16 tightly. It didn't take long for the guard to confirm their identities and was quick to realize his mistake when he said the logs showed six left on patrol and questioned why there were only four in the truck on their return. Red faced, the guard waved them through the gate and returned to his post in the tower, but not before Frank Simmons tore him a new asshole.

Aaron was already out of the truck before Simmons even placed the transmission in park in front of the Special Operation Force Recon tent lines. He started grabbing gear from the truck bed and said he was headed to eat before getting checked out by the medics. Nella suggested he shower too which caused him to sniff his pits and make a face of disgust. Nella followed Aaron with the rest of the teams gear while Simmons lit a cigarette and told Henry he was off to find a medic to give him a once over. Henry grabbed his rifle and water bottle and made his way into the SOFREC tent lines. He peeled off his chest rig and plate carrier and laid them at the foot of the cot neatly. He always liked to keep his gear neat. Lifting his shirt revealed some bruises on his ribs and a hastily patched wound on his left side to match his bullet-hole scar on his chest that he got back in Afghanistan. He tossed his shirt into a green netted laundry bag and pulled a new one out from his barracks box along with a complete change of clothes, placing them next to his chest rig. As he sat down on his cot, the tent flap whipped open and Simmons ducked in with a medic in tow.

The medic immediately grabbed a set of latex medical gloves from his pack and began to pull the blood-soaked Israeli bandage off of Henry. Once the bandage was removed, the medic wiped the wound with an antiseptic wipe. "The wound's just a graze and it should heal quickly on its own," the medic said to Henry. He cleaned the wound area a little more and placed a new bandage on.

"Colonel Howard's on the way here," Simmons said.

"Good, I'd like to stay sit…ow…sitting here," Henry recoiled at the pain.

"Like I said, just a graze," the medic said, snapping his gloves off as he stood up. "Keep it clean, take some Advil, grab a shower, some grub and some rack and you'll be right as rain." The medic picked up his pack and cinched it tight on his shoulders as he walked to the entrance flap. No sooner had the medic left, Colonel Howard ducked into the tent.

"Major Carson," he said.

"Sir," Henry nodded. He would have stood and saluted, but his side hurt so he hoped that and his long standing relationship with Howard would let it slide. He at least sat up a little more straight.

"What the fuck happened out there?" Howard asked rather pointedly. Henry and Simmons took turns debriefing Colonel Howard, filling in the gaps in their stories with the information that Nella and Aaron had told them. By the time they had finished updating Howard, Nella and Aaron had returned to the tent and joined the discussion. "You say you neutralized a few

WMA soldiers before you made it out and one was named Holyfield?" Howard confirmed with them.

"Yes Sir," Nella replied. "I didn't think about it at the time, but do you think he was related to Lilith Holyfield?"

"Most likely," he said without hesitation. "There's no way that this is a coincidence. I better get back to the CP tent. You lot get yourselves squared away, fed and rested."

"Sir," they all said in unison.

***

The chicken was bland, but damn if it wasn't the best thing that Henry had eaten in a long time. Simmons added an unhealthy dousing of salt to his plate and shoveled some broccoli into his mouth. Aaron finished his meal quicker than the rest because he wanted to go to the armories to see about a replacement for his PKM machine gun that he lost in the city. Nella sat quietly in thought, shifting broccoli around her plate with her fork. She brought a piece to her mouth and then placed it back on the plate. Henry and Simmons could tell something was wrong with her, but they were hesitant to ask at first. Finally, after a moment of contemplation, Henry asked her how she was doing which caused her to break down into tears. Henry said he was sorry and that he didn't mean to upset her. She took a deep breath and wiped her eyes. "It's okay," she said, I'm just worried about Brynn and William. Do you think they're okay? I can't believe we just left them there. We're going back, right? To get them?" She took another deep breath. "I need some air." She stormed out before Henry or Simmons could respond.

CHAPTER 10

July 29th, 2021

Las Vegas, Nevada

Dunk and Brynn slipped quietly down the lower level service corridor. The lights were mostly burnt out and the ones that weren't would flicker sporadically. Dunk gripped the Colt 1911 in his hands as they moved. I knew it was a 1911, Brynn had said to herself. The damp air of the corridor surrounded them. There was a leaky pipe somewhere, but they couldn't see it. The *drip drip drip* of water splashing the concrete floor echoed down the narrow hallway. Dunk stopped and held up his closed right fist in a halt sign. Brynn moved in tight behind him and placed her hand on his back. Her wrists were tender from the zip-ties and her face stung from the lumps she had taken at the hands of Sheena and Sofia. Those bitches, Dunk had said in the room before he freed her. They *were* bitches, she thought. A part of her, deep down inside was tempted to wrestle the 1911 from Dunk and turn back to wait for them in her chair, but her more logical self, the former lawyer in her, thought better of that plan. Dunk waved his right hand forward and began to move. Brynn followed without hesitation. Laughter from a room on the left startled Brynn. Dunk spun to aim his pistol at the door. The laughter turned to a dull muffled conversation but the door never opened. They continued towards the end of the corridor where a door marked *Stairs to Street Level* sat tucked behind a neatly stacked pile of dusty wooden skids, blocking their path. Dunk holstered his pistol and quietly began to move the top skid, placing it out of the way. The wood creaked as it scraped along the floor. Brynn tried to help with the next one, but a pain shot through her wrists causing her to drop her side. Dunk managed to take up the weight and move it himself.

Five minutes later, Dunk was dusting off his hands and pushing the door open. The city was darker than she remembered when they were scouting it a few days prior, but at the same time it seemed bright to her eyes. Eyes that had been in the dark for how long now? A day at least she thought, maybe more. It was hard to tell when you're sleep deprived and being beaten and interrogated every few moments. An engine roared to life nearby and stunned Brynn, Dunk and some pigeons. The birds took to the sky and darted quickly out of sight.

The pair moved hastily down a road marked Bellagio Service Road and were headed towards the nearby highway when a pair of headlights turned a corner towards them, shining brightly down the otherwise black laneway. Brynn was quick to take to cover, but Dunk stood still moving only slightly to shield his un-holstered pistol from view. A dark green or black Humvee slowed to a crawl and stopped ten feet from Dunk, who was now holding his right hand over his eyes like a baseball cap brim to block some of the bright light. Two men hopped out of the Humvee and started to walk towards him. "Fellas," Dunk said.

"Sup, Dunk?" the driver replied.

"What are you doing out here," the other added.

"Just doing some security rounds for the boss lady. It's been a bit of a shit show 'round here these last few days," Dunk said. The two men looked at each other and shifted on their feet.

"You alone?" the driver asked. "Coz we're not supposed to be alone with what's going on and…"

The shots echoed off the buildings and sounded as loud as a civil war cannon in the dark little service road. The two soldiers hit the ground before the ejected casings from Dunk's 1911 did. Smoke was still spilling from the barrel as Dunk holstered the pistol and yelled for Brynn to move. Dunk didn't bother checking on the soldiers. He knew they were dead. He knew from the way they fell that he landed both shots in the T-box. He hated that he knew that. Brynn took a knee next to the recently departed passenger and grabbed his M4, two magazines and his canteen. They jumped into the Humvee and sped off, driving over the bodies of the former WMA soldiers.

***

Brynn pounded back the warm water from the canteen while Dunk finessed the Humvee around the derelict vehicles on the highway. She licked her lips as she replaced the canteen's lid and closed her eyes for what felt like a minute but was actually twenty minutes. She was startled awake when Dunk shut the engine off and she instinctively reached for the M4. Dunk raised his hands as if to say whoa, but the M4 was too long to maneuver in the front seat and Brynn struggled with raising it. Dunk let out a laugh. "Fuck!" Brynn shouted. Her lip cut and swollen to match her eye and nose. Dunk laughed harder. Brynn started to cry.

"Shit, I'm sorry," Dunk said. "Didn't mean to make you cry." His hands were still raised.

"No it's... You didn't. I dunno, I'm just fucking tired and..."

"I get it," he said calmly. His voice was low and comforting. "Listen, why don't you jump in the back and get some rest, we've got a good five to six hours before we reach 51 and..."

"How do you know where to go?" she cut him off.

"I mean, the Federation moves into Nevada and Area 51 was the last Fed base in the west, kind of a no brainer... no?" Brynn pursed her lips, then winced and pressed her hand to them. Bleeding again. She nodded and climbed into the back, taking the M4 with her.

"You'll definitely need that back there," Dunk said. Laughing, he started the engine and pulled back onto the road.

***

July 30th, 2021

Area 51, Nevada

It was early morning and the sun was just starting to peak over the mountains as Henry yawned and sipped on his coffee. For a brief moment, he was transported back to Afghanistan. The orange glow of the sky over the mountains, the way the desert air instantly began to warm up and the hum and smell of diesel engines were all the same. He thought of his return to Outpost Nal, a full two months after he had been shot in the chest. Mostly recovered now, he had some lingering pain when he lifted too much weight or moved rapidly. It was to be expected, but it still pissed him off. Doc Taylor and William Heart greeted him as he walked down the ramp of the LAV III that dropped him off with some supplies. He tossed his pack to the side and went to help offload boxes of rations but Doc Taylor told him to piss off and check in with Sergeant Howard. Henry pursed his lips, but didn't argue. He grabbed his pack, doing his best to hide the tinge of pain radiating in his chest and walked over to the command post tent. The fine desert sand, moon-dust as they called it puffed up in clouds around his feet. The tent flaps were flipped open for air flow and before Henry could get a word out, Jonathan Tremblay all but tackled him. The bear-hug sent pain through Henry's healed wound like a jolt of electricity. He did his best to hide this fact but his face betrayed him. Henry had missed Tremblay while he recovered in the hospital at Kandahar Airfield for nearly two months. His thoughts briefly drifted back to the present, and landed on how badly he had missed Tremblay in the nine months it had been since his death on that fucking bridge in Pittsburgh.

"All right you two, save it for leave," Sergeant Howard said. A lit cigarette hung from his lips. A cigarette always hung from his lips. "Welcome back, Carson. Drop your shit off on your bunk and have Doc give you a once over."

"Sarge, I was given the all clear from the hospital," Henry said. Howard's face gave a look that said I'm glad you're okay, but do what I say. He took a puff of his cigarette.

Henry pulled his shirt back down over his left shoulder and hopped off the wooden make-shift exam table Doc Taylor had in his medical tent. Doc told him he was fine, but can expect to be a little tender for a while. Henry gave him a fist bump and tucked his shirt back in. Doc rummaged through his pack and tossed him a small travel sized bottle of Advil and told him to take as needed. The classic army cure all, Advil, coffee and walking it off.

A few days passed and Henry eased back into the Outpost Nal routine. A few distant firefights, probably between nearby Afghan National Army and the Taliban jolted him awake but all-in-all he was settled back in. He helped in the kitchen tent with coffee prep and dishes and tending to the garbage burn pit. By the fourth day, he went to check on the ammunition stock in the towers and froze when he saw the blood stained wood in the South Tower. The bullet holes still looked fresh, but the blood stains were a dark brown now. His eyes moved from the blood stain that belong to him to the blood stain that belonged to Joshua Maxwell. Henry's heart sank a little. That hurt more than the bullet he took to his chest. Max was so young too.

"Tried to clean it, but you know blood. Shit stains," Tremblay said from the chair in the corner. He was looking through a pair of range finding binoculars, but could see Henry's pause through the corner of his eyes. Henry swallowed the wad of spit that formed in his mouth.

"Yeah, had to get all new combats back in Kandahar, shit ruined mine."

***

The roar of a Humvee snapped Henry back to his morning coffee in the SOFREC tent lines. Frank Simmons stepped out and lit a cigarette. He asked Henry what the commotion was, but Henry was still shaking his thoughts clear. Simmons spotted a SOFREC clerk headed their way and asked him what was going. By then, four more Humvee's had passed by the tents. The clerk stopped in front of Henry. He seemed a little nervous and young, but he was moving with a sense of purpose. "Major Carson, Sir," the clerk said, "Colonel Howard's requested your team at the front gate ASAP, Sir." Simmons asked what was happening but the clerk wasn't sure. He told them the gate spooled up the Quick Reaction Force and then Colonel Howard used the field phone to send him for One Four Delta but otherwise didn't know what was going on. The clerk nodded and then left. Simmons took a long haul on his cigarette and tossed it into the butt can a few feet away. Having heard the conversation through the canvas, Nella and Aaron were geared up and exiting the tent. Henry stood, and the four members of One Four Delta made their way to the front gate of Area 51.

The gate was a buzz with Humvee's and soldiers and the M1A1 Abrams tank turret was pointed towards something just beyond the black metal gate. One Four Delta picked up the pace and a Sergeant waved them over. He flipped open a note pad and told Henry that a lone WMA Humvee approached the gate and the occupants asked specifically for him. Aaron pushed passed the Sergeant, nearly knocking him over and ran towards the gate with Henry a few paces behind. The gate opened just enough to allow them through. Aaron had to squeeze his bulk through. The WMA Humvee's headlights where on still, shining brightly in their eyes, but with all of the spot lights from the base Henry could clearly see the two occupants kneeling in front of the Humvee with their hands behind their heads. A large hulking muscular man that Henry didn't know and Brynn Parker.

CHAPTER 11

July 30th, 2021

Las Vegas, Nevada

Lilith Holyfield sat at the oak antique desk that she had brought over from an office building around the corner. It was placed perpendicular to the window of the Bellagio's Penthouse suite that offered once exquisite views of Las Vegas. The view now however, was that of a desolate city with smoke billowing every other block. The artillery and HIMARS rocket barrages had been near constant for a month. Harassing fire Lilith had heard it called when she was in the Central Intelligence Agency. The military would harass the enemy with daily barrages to destabilize and demoralize them before an attack. She had been expecting an attack and when the barrages didn't happen on July 28th, she figured that was it. She was surprised when no attack came and a small recon force was ambushed in the city. She rubbed her temples with her fingers. Her eyes where closed, her fingers were bloody. Outside, a Patriot Missile system fired from a nearby rooftop. The rocket soared through the air and seconds later a boom rattled her windows. Another Federation UAV down. Lilith was thankful they were able to capture a good amount of supplies when they overran a few U.S. Bases. The anti-air systems she acquired has kept any remaining Federation aircraft away from Las Vegas. In fact, the Federation had all but left her alone until they had dealt with Braden Murphy and Khalid Almasi out east. But now, with the east secured, the Federation had the time and resources to focus on her. Lilith opened her eyes.

William Heart sat across from her. Hands bound behind his back and his legs lashed to the wooden legs of the chair. Blood dripped from his face as his head bobbed up and down. The blood spattered on the white marble floor of the Penthouse. A burst of machine gun fire cracking off outside caused him to turn his head. He winced and a string of blood stretched its way down from his mouth to his lap. He blinked at the sunlight shining in through the large Penthouse windows and turned his head back straight. His eyes, blurry from the beatings, could roughly make out the blonde figure across the desk from him. "Br… Brynn…" he stuttered. He couldn't make out her face, but he could see the figure lower its hands to the desk. "Whuh…where am…I?" he asked. No response. A full minute passed and the only sounds in the room were Heart's labored breathing. The blonde figure stood and walked around the desk. Heart could see Lilith clearly now as she sat against the desk in front of him. His heart began to beat faster in his chest as though it were looking for a way out. He pulled on his restraints but it was useless. "Bitch," he said. A spray of blood and spittle burst from his cut lips and embedded in the fibers of Lilith's blue long sleeve shirt. Lilith didn't move.

"Oh William my dear," she said calmly, "I'm not the bitch. Your little friend is. See, if it wasn't for her you might have lived through this." She took a deep breath and scanned Heart's face. He stared daggers back at her, but the shaking in his cheeks told her he was scared. "Now then," she said, pushing herself off the desk, "How long has James Turner been working for the Federation?" she asked. Heart's head cocked slightly to the left as he followed her walk back to her chair. His vision starting to clear slightly.

"Who?" he asked.

"James Turner. How long has he been working for you?"

"I don't know any…" Lilith slammed her fists on the desk, cutting him off.

"Don't fucking lie to me!" she screamed. "I know he fucking defected and that's why he staged that little escape with your god damned Brynn." So, Brynn escaped, Heart thought. A smile drew across his face that sent Lilith into a deeper rage. She grabbed her green-bodied shotgun from the desk and aimed it at Heart's face. Her lips foamed with spit. She was breathing heavy and the shotgun bobbed up and down.

"Mam…" a voice squeaked out from behind Heart and he suddenly realized he had an audience. "M… Maybe we could use him still. Like as a hostage or whatever." The voice was trembling, but seemed to get through to Lilith since she lowered the shotgun.

"A prisoner of war, Sheena," Lilith said. She let out a

breath. "See, it's shit like that that make people think you're stupid." She lowered the shotgun and pursed her lips. "Maybe you're right though. We *can* still use him."

***

The basement maintenance room that once briefly housed Brynn Parker was dark and musty. William Heart strained to see, but his eyes were swelling up again and his vision was blurred because of it. He could hear the faint *drip drip drip* of a leaky pipe somewhere behind him and the occasional *bing* of the elevator as his guard detail rotated out. If he had to guess, it was every hour, but he wasn't certain. He quietly struggled with his arm restraints and could feel them loosen slightly. His wrists were chaffed and raw and blood trickled down to the floor. He stopped moving when he heard the thud of combat boots on the concrete walking toward him. A large muscular blur came into focus carrying a bowl and crouched down in front of him. "Here's some food," Sofia said gruffly. Her voice was deep and flat. She was holding out a bowl of what can only be described as dog food. "Open up." The MP5 slung over her shoulder swung around and clanged against the floor. She turned her

93

head to look and Heart sprang into action.

With all his might he snapped his wrist bindings and threw his head into Sofia's sending the muscular woman backwards while the bowl shattered on the floor. Her nose was broken and bleeding, adding to the already blood-stained concrete. Heart managed to wiggle his legs free and darted for the elevator. At least, he thinks that was the way. He was seeing stars through his blurry eyes after the head-butt. With his arms out, he hit the wall and could see the faint glow of the elevator button. He was breathing heavy and his face stung. His legs felt week, but he would worry about that later. Before he could press the button there was a loud *CRACK* as a round slammed into the concrete wall next to his shoulder. He froze and his heart sank. A witch like cackle filled the room behind him but he didn't move. He stayed frozen, facing the wall.

"Oh fuck, that was good!" Sheena said. She walked forward aiming her Colt 1911 at Heart. A trail of smoke rose from the barrel. "You okay, Sofia?" Sofia grumbled something Heart couldn't hear and got to her feet. He turned slowly to see that blood was pouring from her broken nose, covering her plate carrier that used to belong to Brynn. Sheena and Sofia walked in tandem towards Heart while he fumbled for the elevator button behind his back. The pair were steps away from him when elevator dinged and the door slid open. Heart turned to the open elevator when the cold steel of Sheena's 1911 crashed into the side of his head. Everything went black.

CHAPTER 12

August 1ˢᵗ, 2021

Area 51, Nevada

Brynn shoveled mashed potatoes into her mouth like a kid eating birthday cake. The swelling in her face had gone down, but it still hurt to chew. Little jolts of pain shot from her jaw to the back of her head like electricity arcing on an exposed wire. Butterfly closures held the gash on her face shut as it began to heal. She slurped down some fruit juice that was either mixed berry or blackberry, but she really didn't care what it was because it was delicious. She shredded her chicken with a fork and picked at it until her plate was clean. She was happy to be eating with the team again, though her happiness would quickly fade every time she remembered that William Heart was still somewhere in Las Vegas. She lowered her fork to her plate and choked back some dinner that tried to make a reappearance. That's when she noticed Aaron, Nella and Henry were all staring at her. "I'm doing fine," she said. Her face scrunched up as her tongue searched for a string of chicken stuck in her molars. Henry told her they didn't say anything and Aaron just shook his head. "Will you tell me what happened with Dunk?" she asked. She picked the chicken from her teeth and placed it on her plate.

"Dunk?" Aaron said.

"James Taylor," Henry replied

"Turner," Nella corrected.

"Right, James Turner. He's being held for interrogation. Howard's hoping to get some juicy intel from him for a big OP he's planning." Henry grabbed his coffee and took a sip. Brynn shook her head and told them that Dunk wasn't a threat and that he was the reason she was even alive. She told them again how she escaped, but she knew that they had no say in the matter. She asked what the OP was.

"He calls it Operation Desert Storm three," Nella said, rolling her eyes. Colonel Howard always did love his sequels.

"Original," Brynn said sarcastically.

"Right. Anyway, so the OP's still in the planning stages but the gist is… another few weeks of harassing artillery fire then some targeted strikes followed by a full attack from the East," Henry said quietly.

"What!" Brynn said loudly, "No rescue mission?"

"Currently, no…"

"Bullshit!" Brynn stood up and pointed her hand directly in Henry's face. "You forget that Heart was there for *your* ass in Pittsburgh or what?" It's true. Henry couldn't deny that fact. When he was being held captive by the Republic Sabers in Pittsburgh, William Heart was there taking part in a rescue mission. He'll never forget it. How could he? He owed his life to One Four Delta. And that included Heart.

By now, most of the mess hall had stopped eating and were watching the commotion caused by One Four Delta. Henry pleaded with her to sit down but it was in vain. Brynn was furious. "Fuck this," she shouted and stormed out of the mess hall. Nella shot Henry a look that said *I got this* and went after Brynn.

Aaron looked at Henry, shaking his head. "She's got a

point, ya know."

"I know," Henry said, "I'm working on a plan though."

CHAPTER 13

September 27th, 2021

Area 51, Nevada

Nearly two months had passed since Brynn and Dunk arrived at the Black Gate of Area 51 in their stolen WMA Humvee. And while the month itself was relatively uneventful for One Four Delta, Brynn had been anxious to attempt a rescue mission and had to be forced to stand down more than once. It was hot on September 27th, so Frank Simmons tied open the tent flaps of their tent for airflow. The desert breeze only slightly cooling them. The five of them sat quietly, cleaning their weapons on their cots while *Sabotage* by the *Beastie Boys* played on a beat up Bluetooth speaker. Henry's old iPod Nano had held up surprisingly well over the years. Brynn had been to the armories to replace her MP5 she lost to *'those bitches'* and was issued a Canadian pattern C8 rifle. It was the Canadian Forces equivalent to the U.S. M4 except it was furnished with green plastic instead of black. Brynn swapped out the ELCAN optic for an EOTECH holographic sight and mounted a Surefire fore grip and a PEQ-4 laser. She had spent a few days on the range going over fire positions and fire and move drills with the rifle. The 5.56mm cartridge packed significantly more punch than the 9mm she was used to in the MP5. If they were making a move on the city, there's no room for error she thought and so she practiced diligently.

A few of Brynn's range days were spent with Aaron Walsh. He had asked to join her to test out the M249 SAW he had drawn to replace his PKM that he lost in the city. The 5.56mm round used in the M249 was much more controllable than the 7.62mm round in the PKM, especially to someone of his size. The thing he struggled most with was the fact that the M249 SAW loaded rounds from the left, whereas the PKM loaded on the right but after a few days of solid practice, both dry and with live rounds, Aaron was more than comfortable with the SAW. Henry, Simmons and Nella joined them on their last week of range days so they could practice room clearing, snap shooting and VIP escorting drills. The team was feeling comfortable again and were relatively happy, all things considered. They picked up their casings from the firing points and took a broom to the floor of the plywood house used practice room clearing and once Henry was satisfied that the range was cleared enough, he called One Four Delta to a huddle. He was ready to share his plan.

***

James 'Dunk' Turner smiled when Brynn walked into the interrogation room that had been turned into a makeshift cell for him. She brought him a cheeseburger and fries from the mess hall and placed the plastic tray on the small table in the center of the room. As he scarfed down the meal, Brynn sat on the cot. The burger had ketchup, Dunk hated ketchup, but he didn't complain. It had been years since he had a decent cheeseburger. The room was a dark blue, with a single fluorescent bulb in the ceiling light. The two-way mirror had been reinforced with a chain-fence on the outside but Dunk didn't know that. He wanted to prove he was serious about his defection and never once tried to escape. He probably could have if he wanted to. He was

a big man, and the Federation kept him fairly well fed and hydrat-

ed. Brynn fluffed the cots single thin pillow and placed it behind

her back against the wall. She smiled as Dunk ate. She thought

she may have feelings for him. She felt an overwhelming joy in

his presence. *That's not Stockholm syndrome. He was my savior,* she

thought. Only she didn't think it. She had said it quietly.

"Transference," Dunk said with his mouth full of fries.

"What?" Brynn asked, only now realizing she had actually

spoken.

"It's called transference," he said, "when a person falls

in love with a protector or care giver figure." He sucked some

ketchup off of his thumb.

"I'm not… in love," she said, flush in the face. "How do

you know that anyway?"

"Used to teach Psychology at UC Berkeley after I was dis-

charged from the Marines. Wasn't too bad at it either. And the

pay was decent." Dunk spent the next few minutes telling Brynn

about his former life while he finished off his fries. She sat there

fascinated and listening intently, she had no idea he was more

than a hired goon for Lilith Holyfield. She asked him how he got tangled up in the WMA and he told her the short answer was there were no better options at the time. But, the long answer was that before the Federation pulled together, it was every man for themselves and the best way to survive was to find a crew. "At first, Holyfield was pretty great," he said "She was getting funding from some Irish guy out east, Braden I think his name was, and was working on a plan to rebuild the city. But then she started to change. I'm pretty sure the power started to go to her head and she started hiding assets from this Braden guy. Anyway, he found out and wasn't happy, so he sent a force to get us in line. He wasn't expecting her to obliterate his force. The CIA trained her well, and she's incredibly smart to boot. The Western Mountain Alliance was born that day, and the final humane piece of Lilith Holyfield died."

Brynn told Dunk about their last year out east and how they spent it fighting against Braden Murphy and his New Boston Front forces. How they lost some good friends, but in the end they eliminated Braden Murphy and secured the Eastern half of North America. Dunk nodded along in amazement.

Henry stood on the other side of the two way mirror observing Dunk and Brynn's conversation. He trusted her judgment, but was still skeptical of this James 'Dunk' Turner guy. Simmons joined him and leaned against the chain-fence covered window. The metal tapped the glass causing Brynn and Dunk to look their way for a moment.

"What do you think?" Simmons asked. His voice had a tone of hesitation in it.

"Jury's still out, but Colonel Howard thinks we can use him."

"How so?"

Henry turned to look at Simmons. "He'll make a good guide. Howard thinks we can slip in during the attack and fuck shit up behind the lines." Simmons pulled a cigarette from the pack he keeps in his left leg cargo pocket and placed it between his lips. He smiled and turned to head back to the tent lines.

"Fuckin'eh," he said.

****

The tents were much hotter than the cool interrogation room turned cell that Dunk was used to, but he was happy to be breathing fresh air again. Henry had taken him to the Base Quartermaster and got him squared away with some bedding, clothes and a plate carrier that had modular pouches for magazines, grenades and supplies. Dunk understood why he wasn't issued a weapon, but he felt naked without one. After all, it had been around a decade now that having a weapon on him twenty-four-seven was practically mandatory. The canvas tent flapped in the light breeze with a deep thumping sound. Despite being a sandy desert base, the tent was exceptionally clean. Some sand trailed along the pallet-skid flooring, but other than that it was nice and well kept. Henry led Dunk to an empty cot and placed the barracks box he had been carrying at the foot. He spent a few seconds making sure it was lined up and wasn't askew. Dunk dropped the netted laundry bags on the cot and smiled at Brynn. She had her C8 cracked open and was brushing the interior with a dirty toothbrush. Lying next to her on the cot was a well-read copy of *Harry Potter and the Prisoner of Azkaban*, her favorite in the series. Aside from Brynn, the tent was empty of people. Henry stood up and nodded approvingly at his placement of the barracks box then walked over to his cot and grabbed the banged up Bluetooth speaker. He flicked the power switch on the back and the speakers crackled to life. He spent the next several minutes trying to find a song and finally Brynn shouted to "Just fucking pick something!" He settled on *Renegades of Funk* by *Rage Against the Machine*.

Mid-way through the song, Simmons, Nella and Aaron ducked into the tent. They had been studying a map of the area surrounding Las Vegas and were arguing about what the best route was. Dunk stood up as they made their way to their respective cots. He was nervous. His knees felt a little weak and the flutter in his stomach confirmed it. He wasn't worried about them hurting him, he wouldn't be standing here if they wanted to hurt him. He worried about what they thought of him. Frank Simmons dropped his M14 rifle on his cot and walked over to Dunk. He got close to him, clearly sizing him up even though Dunk was six-foot-two and a solid two-hundred and forty pounds. Simmons on the other hand was pushing five-foot-ten and one-hundred eighty pounds. He look up at Dunk. Dunk looked down at him.

"Defector," Simmons said. The tent grew silent. An eerie silence like a cemetery at Halloween. A smile grew across Simmons face and he slapped both of Dunk's tree-trunk like biceps with his hands. The tent burst into laughter and Dunk relaxed.

"He grows on you," Nella said. Simmons laughed harder and walked back to his cot. "I'm Nella Saba, that's Aaron Walsh," she said pointing at the other large man in the tent. Aaron smiled a toothy grin through is red wiry beard and popped open the feed tray cover on his M249. He cleared the gun and popped the barrel off to wipe it down. "We're former *defectors*," Nella said, shooting a glare at Simmons. "Used to be part of the Republic Sabers but we got out. Met up with this crew and we've been working to right some wrongs." Dunk felt even more relaxed now. He thought that if they could accept *them*, then as long as he proves his worth he'll be just fine.

Henry turned the iPod and speaker off and packed them away in his barracks box. He got up and walked over to close the tent flaps on the once side, tapping Simmons who had just stepped out to smoke, on the arm. Simmons tossed the butt in the nearby can and exhaled a cloud of smoke as he ducked back into the tent. The tent had gone quiet and the only sounds were coming from Aaron's M249 as he locked the barrel back into place and cycled the action a few times. It was well oiled and smooth. Henry pulled out a map of Las Vegas and his collapsible map pointer and began to detail the plan. "We're rolling out early and heading west," the pointer slid across the map. "At oh-seven-hundred hours, the 49th Field Artillery will launch a barrage from the North consisting of M777 Howitzers, HIMARS rockets and whatever else they can throw. Their objective is to try and cripple WMA Anti-Air because Colonel Howard has a small surprise. While that is happening, the 4th Armored and the 221st Cavalry will move on the city from the east, escorted by the 40th Infantry and 1 PPCLI." Henry paused and looked around.

"What's our objective?" Nella asked.

"We know the objective, what's the fuckin surprise!" Aaron said excitedly.

"Not sure, but Howard said it's good. The objective is the same as always. Infiltrate and eliminate. Any more questions?" Henry asked.

"Wheels?" Simmons asked.

"Oh, you'll love them," Henry said smiling.

CHAPTER 14

October 4th, 2021

Las Vegas, Nevada

The WMA insignia had been stripped from the Humvee that Brynn and Dunk had turned up in at Area 51 but the black paint was left to allow One Four Delta to blend in better as they made their way into Las Vegas. A Browning .50 caliber machine gun had been added to the roof, which Aaron happily stood at and manned while the vehicle bounced across the rough terrain. The smile on Simmons face stretched from ear to ear as he slowed down to cross a ditch. He always wanted a Humvee. Sure, this belonged to Federation, but for all intents and purposes, it was his. Henry rode shotgun and navigated through the darkness. They drove without lights to avoid detection. It was hard but, if you went slow and had an experienced driver, anything was possible. Still, both Simmons and Henry were relieved when the sun began to rise and visibility was better. Henry directed Simmons to an area of low ground called defilade and halted the Humvee. Defilade kept the vehicle better protected from the enemy by keeping it in low ground and out of site. Henry grabbed a spotter's scope and his G36-C and turned to look at the passengers in the back. Nella, Brynn and Dunk were crammed in the back seat while Aaron stood up through the roof hatch. Henry said to sit tight and relieve Aaron if he needs a break from the gun. The three seated passengers nodded an acknowledgment and Aaron thrust a thumbs up, down from the hatch. While Henry was talking, Simmons had left the Humvee and retrieved a suppressed McMillan TAC-50 from the trunk space and began to walk up the hill. Henry hopped out and followed along.

As they reached the crest of the hill, Simmons and Henry crouched down and slowed their movement, careful not to silhouette themselves on the hill. Simmons paused, went prone and unfolded the bipod of the .50 caliber sniper-rifle, slowly stretching it out in front of him. Henry went prone next to him and the two slowly leopard crawled to the crest of the hill. As soon as they reached the top, Henry unfolded the legs on the spotter's scope, removed the cover and began to get a lay of the land. Simmons adjusted the rifle against his shoulder, then removed it. He brushed some rocks away from his elbow rests and reset the rifle into its position. Henry peered through the scope and quietly watched the two guards of the western tower talking to each other. They were sitting in chairs, *bonus*, Henry thought. He pressed a button on the right side of the scope. It made a faint click as it reset. The scope, doing its job, displayed the distance to the tower guard on the left. "Left target. Range, 1672 meters," Henry said. Simmons reached over the scope of his rifle with his left hand and adjusted a dial. *Click click click.* "Wind, 2 clicks west to east." *Double bonus.* Henry did his best Moff Tarkin impression, "You may fire when ready." Simmons smirked and called him a nerd. The pot calling the kettle black. Simmons took a few breaths in and out. In and out. In… and… out. He toggled the safety on the rifle, flipping it from safe to fire. The audible click sounded as loud as a car crash in the rel-ative silence on the hill. Another breath in. And out. The pad of his index finger deformed in his glove as Simmons pulled the trigger. The .50 caliber round exploded from the suppressed barrel sending a cloud of dust and small rocks a foot into the air around them. Through the scope, Henry could see the faint glow of the back of the round and the shockwave trail marking its path through the air. It felt like slow motion, but the bullet was traveling 823 meters per second. Tearing through the air as it started to drop, descending on its target. They couldn't hear it from their perch on the hill, but they knew the sound it made when the bullet passed through the guards throat. A sickening wet *thwap*. Simmons worked the bolt, ejecting the spent casing and chambering another round. The guard on the right barely had time to react. His face splattered with blood and tissue from the man who was sitting next to him, now slumped over in his chair, what used to be his head painted the wall and ceiling of the tower like a Jackson Pollock painting. A second .50 caliber round ripped through the air as Simmons pulled the trigger. The guard had just managed to stand up. The round took him square in the chest. His plate carrier exploded in a puff of smoke and dust. Plate carriers were great at stopping most rounds, but not a .50 caliber. The bullet tore through him, followed by bits of ceramic and fabric from the carrier. The guard dropped in a heap on the floor of the tower, blood pooling underneath him.

"Targets down," Henry said. Simmons ejected the casing and chambered another round. They waited, patiently. After a few minutes, no other guards appeared, no back-up arrived at the gate and they weren't being shot at. Simmons toggled the safety on the rifle to safe, Henry packed away the spotter's scope and they quietly headed back to the Humvee.

***

Lilith Holyfield shot out of her bed in the Bellagio's Penthouse suite when the concussion of an explosion rocked the building. The crystals in the dining area chandelier were clinking together and Lilith's prized bottles of scotch rattled on the shelf. She was wearing a pair of black bike shorts but no top. She grabbed the shotgun from the rack next to her bed and rushed out to the main living area. A second explosion shook the building and the smoke trail of an anti-air missile lingered outside of her window. The sun was rising and the sky was a fiery orange colour. She pressed her left hand to the glass and stood looking out over the Las Vegas Strip. Two more explosions went off further away, then another two and another two. Smoke was rising throughout the city. She could see the Air Defense system on the roof of the Paris Hotel begin to swivel when it was suddenly engulfed in smoke and flame. Secondary explosions shook the windows as the missiles in the Air Defense system cooked off and exploded on the roof. Lilith slammed her left fist on the glass. She watched as four Humvee's and an Armored Personnel Carrier raced down the Strip dodging the remains of the Eiffel Tower that fell all those years ago. More Air Defense rockets streaked into the sky as even more explosions tore through the buildings. Her soldiers on the street levels were scrambling for cover. Two men dove into a checkpoint tower in front of the Bellagio where another two men were already taking cover. A moment later the tower suffered a direct hit from a 155mm Artillery shell, obliterating it and its occupants. Lilith stood in her suite, frozen. A feeling of utter helplessness washed over her like a tsunami. If it were possible, her pale skin were even paler. Sofia and Sheena burst into the suite frantically, they had their weapons up at the ready. Lilith spun, shotgun in hand, and as she did one of the final Air Defense systems was struck. The flash of the blast silhouetted her like she was on the poster of an action movie. Only this wasn't a movie.

Sofia darted into the bedroom quickly and came back with a set of clothes she pulled from a chest of drawers. The black glossy chest held Lilith's clothes all laid out neatly folded in rows of corresponding articles. Bras and underwear on top, t-shirts in the middle and pants on the bottom. Sofia handed them to Lilith who was still in a state of shock. Explosions continued to rock the Strip. "Mam, we've got to get you down to the basement. The Observation Post on the northern edge of the city reported a mass of armor and infantry headed this way." Lilith grabbed the clothes and started to get dressed. Sheena, her purple hair roughed up like bed-head instead of its usual well-kept swoop told Lilith that they had lost contact with the Observation Posts on the North, West and East edges of the city. Lilith's pale face was now turning a shade of fire engine red as she zipped up her pants and walked over to where she kept her boots and plate carrier.

"Why did the posts wait so long to report a column of fuckin' armor?" Lilith asked as she cinched the plate carrier tight.

"We're not sure mam," Sofia said, "but I have a feeling that traitor Turner squealed."

"Sheena, go down and shore up the defenses. I want sniper teams in the towers and move what artillery and anti-tank weapons we have to the north. Sofia, you're with me."

***

The Humvee approached the western gate and slowed to a crawl. Decaying garbage crunched up under the run-flat tires as they came to a halt ten meters in front of the gate. Aaron Walsh scanned for targets behind the .50 cal. He swiveled the gun slowly from side to side. His eyes darted to the tower, then to the gate, then to the roof tops and windows of the nearby buildings. For a moment, One Four Delta sat quietly in the vehicle. Watching. Waiting. Listening. A minute felt like an eternity and finally Henry Carson cleared his throat. His heart was pounding so hard it felt as though it were jumping up to the back of his throat and choke him there in his seat. "You're up," he said flatly. Nella Saba opened the door to the Humvee and hopped out. She raised her M4 and began to scan for threats. James 'Dunk' Turned nodded and squeezed his six-foot-two bulk out of the door behind her. The sun was almost fully over the eastern mountains now and the heat was starting to bake the garbage on the ground. The stench was foul, like the bottom of a fast food garbage can that never saw a bag. Henry and Brynn exited the vehicle next and slowly moved to the right side of the gate, weapons at the ready.

Nella followed Dunk as he headed towards the base of the tower. Blood from the two guards had begun to drip through the wooden floor boards up top and made a thick plopping sound as it splashed in a puddle on the asphalt. Dunk reached the base of the tower and paused. Nella moved up to the opening. It was an opening in the base of the tower similar to a drive-thru window. It was protected by a stack of waist high sand bags that were stacked three deep. Nella slid the barrel of her M4 into the opening as she leaned in to clear the area. *Drip drip drip.* Nothing but the sound of thick blood escaping its former owner. Nella hopped the sand bags followed closely by Dunk who made his way to the tower stairs. He told her the gate controls were up top. She scanned down the road while he climbed the stairs. The wooden steps groaned under his weight. Nella could hear the click of a button, but nothing was happening. She looked up and Dunk leaned over the sandbag wall of the towers back. "Power's out," he said.

"Fuck," she grumbled. Nella lowered her M4 and looked around. Her black combat boot kicked something as she turned. A thick black cable, like a large snake lay along the garbage filled gutter of the road. She traced the cable with her eyes until they landed on a generator. She walked over, slung her M4 across her chest and knelt next to it. The life blood of the generator, precious diesel fuel, was leaking out and pooling around the base. The smell reminded her of an old gas station, an army base and a parking lot all at once. She ran the index finger on her right hand around the gaping bullet hole in the generator. "It's toast," she said over her shoulder. The glimpse of a weapon in her peripherals sent a jolt of fear down her spine. She sprang to her feet and spun around, raising her M4. The plastic hand guards creaked as she grasped them with a strong grip. She was aiming at Dunk who was at the bottom of the stairs with a KRISS Vector sub-machine gun slung over his shoulder. She told him to drop it and he froze in place. He raised his hands slowly and did as she asked. Henry asked what was happening from the other side of the gate but Nella was too focused on Dunk to respond.

Henry sprinted to the opening in the tower and vaulted the sand bags like an athlete jumping hurdles. Brynn was hot on his heels. The blood from the tower guards had mostly stopped dripping now and had formed a large puddle on the cement that splattered when they ran through it. They saw Dunk standing there with his hands raised while Nella had her M4 raised. Henry pointed his G36-C at Dunk and began to circle around to the front of him. Brynn raised her C8 and aimed it at Nella. The tension between them was thick enough to cut with a butter knife. The sun was fully over the eastern mountains now and the air was heating up. Sweat beaded on their foreheads as they stood there, like a stand-off in an old gangster movie. Henry took a step forward and was about to speak when Nella lowered her rifle. She told them what happened with Dunk and the gun. Henry lowered his rifle, slowly. Brynn kept her aim.

Dunk continued to stand there, hands in the air. "I get it," he said, "I really get it. But listen, I'm on your side. And I'd feel a lot safer rolling up to Casa De Holyfield with a piece." Henry slung his rifle, crouched down and picked up the KRISS Vector on the ground. It was well used, but clean and in good condition. The bluing on the metal was worn in areas, but there was no rust or other damage. Henry removed the magazine and ejected the .45 ACP round from the chamber into his hand. The chamber look good too. He clicked the round back into the magazine which he then loaded back into the gun. Nella stood shocked when Henry handed the Vector back to Dunk.

"He's got a point," Henry said. "He's risking his biscuits coming back with us and if Brynn trusts him… so do I." Brynn lowered her rifle and a smile grew across her face. The fresh scar on her cheek wrinkled.

Nella was uneasy as the four of them grabbed on to the gate and pushed it open. She hoped Henry knew what he was doing. Once Simmons rolled the Humvee through the gate, Henry, Brynn and Dunk got in. Nella took a deep breath and hopped in last.

***

His head was all but split open. The pain was excruciating. Like a million needles stabbing him anywhere they could. He wished he would lose consciousness, or death would be even better. The beatings had become more intense and more regular lately. But William Heart held strong and refused to give any information other than his name, rank, favourite colour, favourite food and what kind of animal he would like to be. A turtle, not that anyone ever asked him. But now, his fingers were all broken, his head gouged and bleeding, his face puffy and his stomach panged with a burning hunger. He hadn't eaten in so long he couldn't remember what his last meal was. Another punch to the face rocked his head back and the wooden blood stained chair tipped over. Heart landed on his back with a thud that took the wind out of him. His head bounced off the floor but he was already in so much pain he barley felt it. Despite his appearance and current situation, he was proud of himself. Torture had been the worst thing he has ever experienced and he was yet to crack. Other than crack a joke. He laughed out loud as he lay on his back. His laugh turned to a cough and he spit some blood into the air.

The laughter filled Sofia Hernandez with a rage she could barely control. She stood Heart and his chair back up, her biceps bulged as she lifted him. Sweat dripped off her angry furrowed brow. She took a few paces in front of him and turned sharply, firing her blood and spit covered combat boot into his chest, knocking him over again. Sofia stood over top of him, grabbed the front of his shirt and lifted him off the floor again. She cocked her right arm back, stiffened her muscles and formed a fist. He burst into laughter again. She shot her fist forward into his face and cracked his two front teeth exposing the nerves. She released her grip and let him slump on the floor. The unconscious embrace he had wished for was finally gifted to him. "I feel better," she said.

Sofia turned to look at Commander Lilith Holyfield who was leaning against a table smoking a cigarette. Lilith's eyes had a hint of panic behind them. Sofia asked if she was okay. Lilith told her she was, but she wasn't really. She had hoped to gain even a slight idea of the Federation's plan from her prisoner, but he gave her nothing. Absolutely nothing. Her Outposts around the city were no longer reporting in and the most concerning was the destruction of her air defense systems. Almost as soon as the last one was destroyed the sky above Las Vegas was abuzz with Unmanned Aerial Vehicles that were feeding information to the Federation. Information that she had no real way to counter. She was almost down to the filter of her cigarette when she flicked it to the side. She stood up from the table and walked over to her prisoner. He was out like a light. Head slumped to the side, mouth gaped open. Bloody spit dribbled from what used to be lips. Lilith grabbed him by the hair and raised his head. He didn't stir. She looked him over and released her handful of greasy, unwashed, blood matted hair. His head slumped back over. He still didn't stir. Lilith stood up straight and took a deep breath. She knew she wasn't going to get anything out of William Heart. He was useless to her now. She stared at him for a moment before finally speaking. "String him up."

CHAPTER 15

October 4th, 2021

Las Vegas, Nevada

The buildings shook and their windows rattled as the Federation tanks, Armored Personnel Carriers and Infantry Fighting Vehicles pushed slowly into the city. Derelict and burnt out vehicles littered the streets creating a zig-zagging maze to navigate. The M1A1 Abrams tank tracks had no issues rolling over the vehicles, crushing them under their monstrous sixty-ton weight. The sight of the 4th Armored Division rolling into Las Vegas was nothing short of captivating. The tanks were behemoths that dominated the road and made the APC's and IFV's behind them look like hot wheels. Dismounted Infantry from 1 PPLCI formerly housed in Alberta, Canada, swept through buildings that flanked the streets to clear out any potential threats and offer extra protection to the vehicles. So far, the drive in from the east had been relatively calm for the massive Federation force. Four dismounted soldiers were wounded by a sniper and three were killed. One APC had an engine failure causing the soldiers to have to dismount and walk. The column took some fire from a small team of WMA soldiers in their first minute inside city limits but the lead tanks 120mm cannon removed any trace of them from the planet.

Colonel Howard stood proudly in the Crew Commanders position of a Stryker IFV. He peered over the top of the turret, taking in the surroundings and guiding the column by instructions over the radio. He thought back to his time in Afghanistan commanding the LAV III that took him, Henry Carson, Jonathan Tremblay, William Heart, Doc Taylor, Jason Field and Joshua Maxwell across the arid landscapes of the Panjwai District. Howard was brought back to reality as they turned off of Tropicana Avenue into the abandoned landing strip of the former McCarran International Airport, which they intended to use as a staging area, but that's when things took a turn for the worse.

The explosion was enormous and absolutely rocked the vehicles nearby. The turret of the lead M1A1 Abrams tanks soared through the air and landed nearly fifty meters to its left. Flames poured out of every hole they could find in the vehicle. Before Howard could react, a second explosion rocked the convoy as the second tank in line met the same fate as the first. Howard grabbed the radio switch and screamed into the headset, "Fan the fuck out! Did anyone see a fire point? What was it?" Vehicles began to jockey into positions on the airfield as infantry took cover behind burnt out cars and in buildings. Tanks from the rear raced to the front. Howard almost missed it, but at the last second, he saw what he's sure was a Javelin anti-tank missile dive into the turret roof of the third tank. The turret stayed on this one, but flames shot up into the sky through the hatches, cooking the crew alive like a flame grilled barbeque. He's not sure if anyone saw the firing point, but a few of the tanks opened fire. Blasting the airport and surrounding buildings with 120mm tank high explosive rounds and peppering overturned vehicles with their roof mounted machine guns. An RPG screamed by the fourth tank, missing its rear by inches. It skipped off the hot airfield asphalt and soared off into the sky before detonating well away from any Federation soldiers. The cloud of dust kicked up on the roof by the RPG firing betrayed its operator's position and the tank gunner was easily able to spot the location. The gunner swiveled the turret around and fired. The High Explosive round slammed into the corner of the building's roof, deleting any trace of the RPG soldier and anyone within five meters of him. Rubble from the building crumbled down to the ground like a rockslide on a mountain hill.

All hell broke loose. As the vehicles and infantry pressed forward towards the airport, WMA soldiers from all around opened fire with everything from snipers and assault rifles to machine guns and anti-armor weapons. Howard was stunned by the absolute chaos of it all. Machine gun rounds cracked all around him. Some skipped off the front fascia of the vehicle, kicking up dust and sparks in their wake. Some slammed into the turret. One round soared inches over his head and thumped into the radio mast with an audible metallic knock. His body recoiled into the IFV on instinct. Had that round been on target, ducking wouldn't have done him any good. He stood back up as an APC erupted in flame and smoke off to his left, the heat from the explosion singed the stubble on his cheeks. The troops, eleven of them, poured out of the back of the APC in a panic. Howard felt a sense of terror when he saw they were on fire. He watched as they were cut down by machine gun fire as they rolled around in an attempt to put out the flames.

THUNK THUNK THUNK. An IFV next to him fired three rounds from its 25mm Bushmaster cannon. An RPG tore through the air between them it smoke trail hung in midair like a dirty cloud. Howard saw the fire point come from an old city bus and directed the gunner of his vehicle on target. Three 25mm rounds ripped into the bus, eliminating another RPG. *Move forward*, he thought. *We have to move!* He barked orders into his radio headset and within moments the vehicles began to move closer towards the airport buildings. WMA soldiers scrambled from their cover on the airfield as tanks rolled over the burnt remains of airport vehicles. Once close enough, Federation infantry dismounted their APCs and began to sweep through the surrounding buildings. It didn't take long. Half an hour at most. But it felt like hours. Combat had a way of changing a person's perception of time. Howard remained in his IFV and continued to maneuver the vehicles like a professional chess player in a world championship tournament. Once Howard was satisfied that all threats from the airport had been eliminated, the Federation vehicles consolidated on the far side of the airport. The Las Vegas Strip was in view.

***

"Get that fucking 82 set up!" Sheena Edwards screamed. Two soldiers carrying an 82mm recoilless rifle and tripod mount jogged over towards a hastily built position made of sandbags. They laid the mount and rested the long green tube of the rifle on it, locking it in place with a linchpin. Sheena turned around and ordered a machine gunner to move positions from an overturned pickup truck to a sandbagged position further up the road. Explosions from the direction of the airport shook the glass windows around them. Distant smoke plumes filled the sky putting a smile on Sheena's face. Four Humvee's and an M1 Abrams tank approached her position from the rear. Sheena walked to the tank, slung her M4 across her back and climbed up onto the turret. The WMA had been able to secure a small handful of six older M1 Abrams tanks a few years prior, but were unable to maintain them properly. The Abrams was notoriously needy in terms of upkeep. Sheena was able to siphon enough fuel to keep one on the move, but the remaining five where positioned on the Strip to guard the Bellagio Head Quarters should it ever be needed. She leaned on the barrel to talk with the commander of the tank. He was an older man and his beard was peppered with grey and black. Wrinkles surrounded his eyes as he squinted in the sunlight. He rested his arms on the roof of the turret while he confirmed the plan with Sheena. He was nervous and she could tell. She was nervous too, but did her best to hide this fact from him. Small arms rounds began to crack over head as the airport battle intensified. The explosions rattled everything in the area. Sheena ordered the tank commander to press further up the Strip towards the remains of the Luxor Casino, the former black pyramid was now dirty brown and crumbling, closely resembling its counterparts in Egypt. "Once there, back into the corner, down the alley. Once they push this way, I'll need you to attack from the rear. I'll also have a few anti-armor positions back there with some ground support," she said with impressive authority. The tank commander shot her a thumbs up and ordered the driver to move. Sheena hopped off the tank, landing with a thump on the road, setting off to confirm her defenses were set.

The sounds of the airport battle began to quiet and Sheena grew tenser. Sweat ran from her purple hair as she worked to ensure the Strip was well defended. She had one thousand soldiers at her disposal which she has placed around the Strip in buildings, along rooftops and the road. Most of the soldiers were armed with rifles, shotguns and pistols but she had ten remaining anti-armor teams, just over a dozen machine gunners and one man-portable air defense unit. For vehicles, there was one M1 Abrams parked by the Luxor and five scattered down the Strip to guard the Bellagio, three APC's armed with .50 caliber machine guns in the turrets and thirty Humvee's, half of which had .50 caliber guns mounted on them and the other half were just transports.

Sheena stood on the remains of an overhead pedestrian crossing and surveyed the situation. Below her, Humvee's pushed old vehicles around to create blockades and delivered troops and ammunition to the front line. She had been so focused on shoring up defenses that she hadn't realized that reports of fighting from the airport had stopped coming in. Her radio crackled with life and the voice of Commander Lilith Holyfield sternly asked her for a situation report. Sheena, as confidentially as she could, replied that defenses were set and the strike teams at the airport were engaged. It was then that she realized that she hadn't heard from the strike teams in a while and a wave of panic washed over her like a tidal wave. Sheena sprinted down the stairs, ignoring her radio and ran to the nearest Humvee. She hopped into the back, slamming the door while ordering the driver to head towards the observation post on top of the MGM Grand Casino. Commander Holyfield continued to bark into the radio to get her attention. Sheena pressed the button on her radio, "Wait one," she said angrily.

"Don't you DARE FUCKING TELL M…" Sheena angrily turned the radio's power switch to off, silencing Lilith's voice. The driver of the Humvee looked nervously at her through the rearview mirror. *I'll pay for that later*, Sheena thought.

A few moments later, the Humvee pulled into the casino through the missing front entrance doors and Sheena hopped out, making her way to the top floor. She was glad the elevator still worked even though the adrenaline surging through her would have gotten her up the stairs. She flung the rooftop doors open and approached the two-person sniper team who were laying prone in the observation post. She slowly laid down next to the man holding a spotter's scope and asked him for an update. He was a younger man, probably in his mid-twenties. Sheena noticed that his hands were trembling as he moved the scope over to her. The woman behind the sniper rifle barely moved. She could have been a mannequin if Sheena hadn't heard her clear her throat. Positioning the scope in front of her eye, Sheena took in the sight of the airport. The tidal wave of fear made landfall again as she watched the Federation vehicles consolidating and reorganizing themselves to continue their push into the city. She began to count and the spotter diligently jotted what she said down in his field pad. She counted fifteen M1A1 Abrams tanks, ten Infantry Fighting Vehicles and twenty Armored Personnel Carriers. She wasn't able to get a number on soldiers so the spotter noted 'a fuck-load'.

"Why aren't they moving?" the woman on the rifle asked. Sheena was surprised at how meek her voice was. She moved the spotter's scope around and observed that the vehicles were indeed not moving, but what was really strange was that the troops were taking cover. It was then that the skies ripped open and began to roar like a lion.

CHAPTER 16

October 4th, 2021

Las Vegas, Nevada

Lilith Holyfield and Sofia Hernandez stood quietly in the elevator. Neither of them spoke or made a sound while the small box lifted them to the top of the Bellagio. William Heart sat, tied to his chair, in front of them. He was much more vocal than them. Letting out groans and gasps and the occasional 'fuck you' when he could muster the strength. The copper metallic flavor of blood filled his mouth from his cracked teeth and split lips. He tried to spit it out, but the pain was unbearable. He let it dribble from the bruised corners of his mouth. Not caring that it was covering his shirt. His head felt as though it weighed a thousand pounds, bobbing back and forth on his aching neck. He had never wished for death before. Not once. But in that moment, in the elevator, William Heart wished for death.

The elevator began to slow and then stopped with a jerk that jolted another wave of pain through Heart. The doors dinged as they opened, revealing a long grey hallway that was empty except for an old wet floor sign that lay flat on the tile as though someone had knocked it over. A layer of dust caked the area. Heart groaned as Sofia pushed his chair forward. The small metallic wheels click-clacked on the tile like a toy train. They paused at the wet floor sign and Lilith stepped forward to move it. Heart flexed with all the strength he had left, but it was useless. His feeble attempt to break his restraints failed. Hope for escape faded from his mind. Sofia caught his escape attempt in her peripherals and laughed as she pushed the chair forward once the way was clear. The hallway turned to the left in a sharp angle and then again to the right. Signs on the doors told Heart this was where the former Casino's server rooms lived and he tried to figure out what their plan for him was as his chair rolled over the dusty grey tile. The hallway came to an end with a dark grey door with a cracked window. The bright noon sunlight poured through the glass, lighting the otherwise desolate hall.

The three of them stopped at the door and Lilith pushed it open with a grunt. The door creaked and groaned as it swung open. It was evident that it had been a while since anyone had been up on this roof. The sun assaulted Hearts eyes as his chair moved out onto the roof, like a flashbang detonating in a room. The warm desert air blasted his face as they moved across the rooftop. He could hear nearby explosions and the occasional zip and crack of bullets that completely missed their intended targets. His heart raced like a thoroughbred horse galloping on a track. Still attempting to figure out what they were doing on the roof, his eyes darted from Lilith, up to plumes of smoke in the north skyline and down to the edge of the building that was rapidly approaching.

Lilith grabbed two lengths of ropes that were coiled up on the sandy roof top. She moved casually as though she were working on a job site. She tied an end of one of the lengths to the guard railing of the building. She did the same to the other length, cinching the knots tightly. Satisfied, she turned to face Heart with a smile that was beautiful but sinister at the same time. She held the untied ends of the ropes in her hands bounc-

ing them up and down like the reigns of a horse she was riding

down a mountain trail.

Sofia cut the bindings on Hearts wrists with her knife and

stepped back as though she were saying he was free to go. Heart

didn't try to leave. He was in too much pain from his torture, not

to mention malnourished and dehydrated from a lack of proper

diet. He slowly brought his wrists around in front of him and

began to rub the raw skin and open wounds left behind from

constant bondage. It felt good to rub away some of the pain.

He started to relax a little, forgetting he was still on the roof.

Still sitting in front of the Commander of the WMA, who had

spent the last month interrogating him, who had probably killed

Brynn. *Oh god. Brynn*, he thought. His hands began to tremble

as he looked up at Lilith. She had moved close to him now and

was crouched down, face-to-face with him on the Bellagio's hot

roof. Her sinisterly beautiful smile sent fear shooting through

his spine like jolts of electricity causing the hairs on his neck to

stand at attention. She tied an end of rope to his right wrist. It

hurt. She tied the other rope to his left. It *hurt*. The nearby

explosions and gunfire from the airport battle had subsided, but

Heart didn't notice. He was too focused on what was happening on the roof. His gaze darted back and forth from his wrists, to the guard rail as he worked out Lilith's plan.

"Anything you wish to get off your chest," Lilith said. Her smile had faded.

"Go fuck yourself," Heart said, spitting some clotted blood at her.

"Sofia," Lilith said, waving her hand forward as she stepped out of the way.

Sofia grabbed Heart by the scruff of the neck and hauled him to his feet with her bulk. He was light in her arm. She pushed him forward and he stumbled. His legs were weak. She stood him up again and pushed forward to the edge. Heart peered over the railing. It didn't look that far down through his blurred eyes, but he wasn't going all the way down. Sofia raised him up onto the edge. His legs tremored as though there were an earthquake. His heart jumping into his throat trying to make the leap for him.

Lilith walked up behind him and drew a deep breath that told Heart she was about to say something. He mustered all the strength his voice had left and yelled, "GO FUCK YOUR-

SELF!" Lilith responded with a push to the small of his sweat drenched back.

The fall was brief, about ten feet. But to Heart it felt like a kilometer. As he fell his thoughts raced to cover his life. He saw his family, his section in Afghanistan and One Four Delta. It was true what they say about your life flashing before your eyes. The fall ended with a snap that dislocated his shoulders with a sickening *pop* that severed his brachial arteries. The blood began to fill his chest cavity and within moments, William Heart finally met Death. Lilith and Sofia stood peering over the edge. Satisfied with their message to the Federation and One Four Delta, Lilith grabbed her radio to check in with Sheena. It was then that the skies ripped open and began to roar like a lion.

CHAPTER 17

The Humvee pulled to a stop at a road block near the Stratosphere Tower. The old X-Scream rollercoaster ride swung lightly over the edge like a long metallic flag hanging by the thread of its last remaining safety break. Henry's hands trembled with a nervous energy. They had encountered little resistance as they pushed into the Strip from the western outpost. A small squad of WMA soldiers at a checkpoint were caught off guard as Aaron used the .50 caliber gun to turn them into a fine paste. They took some sniper fire a few moments later. The round tore into the ammo can on the .50cal causing Aaron to duck into the Humvee. Simmons cranked the wheel hard to the left and dismounted while the vehicle was still rocking back and forth. His scoped M14 sent a 7.62mm round soaring through the desert air and into the snipers T-box. He was a poor excuse for a sniper. Probably a fucking new guy, Simmons had said to them as he climbed back into the vehicle. The main attack on the eastern edge of the city had drawn most of the WMA fighters that way which made for easy entry into the city. *I love it when a plan comes together.*

Simmons shut the ignition off and climbed out of the vehicle. The rest of One Four Delta took a breath and did the same. Dunk was visibly nervous. His knees shook like a Jell-O mold at an older relatives Christmas dinner party. Thoughts of what Lilith Holyfield would do to him if she caught him. She'd probably string him up from the Bellagio. That is, if he wasn't killed in a firefight first. Taking a deep breath, a feeble attempt to calm down, Dunk lead the team into the Stratosphere, *The Strat*, they called it. There was a gaping hole in the base which made for an easy entry point. The hole looked old, like it had been there for years and it probably had. Likely from the First Battle of Las Vegas when Holyfield took over, they all thought as they passed through the crumbling dusty concrete. Aaron Walsh covered the entrance hole with his M249 while Nella Sabba cleared the lower level of the tower. Henry, Dunk, Simmons and Brynn headed up the tower to do a quick recon of the area.

The stairs were in decent shape for a derelict building. There was cracking and crumbling concrete and some missing steps with exposed rebar, but all things considered, they had seen buildings in worse shape. Brynn led the way, puffing and panting heavily as they climbed. She let her C8 dangle on its sling for a few floors to give her arms a rest, only picking it back up when they neared the top. Henry, Dunk and Simmons huffed and puffed behind her as they climbed. Simmons commented more than once about quitting smoking as he wheezed his way to the top of the tower, but once they reached the summit and after a sip of water, he lit a cigarette and took a long drag before heading to the observation decks. Dunk was showing Brynn some locations of observation posts as Henry watched the plumes of smoke rising from the airport. His spotter's scope shook in his hands making the picture unsteady. Simmons rested the stock of his M14 on the railing and peered through his sight. Henry hadn't thought of that. He unfolded the legs of the scopes and rested them on the railing. *Perfect.*

"Idiot," Simmons said with a chuckle.

"What do you guys see?" Brynn asked inquisitively. The explosions were faint at this distance but the smoke plumes showed clear signs of a battle.

"Not much at the moment. I can see… Jesus… I can see two tanks and an APC down at least," Henry said. His voice faltered as he spoke like a teen entering puberty. Dunk pointed to two more checkpoints that lay ahead as well as the positions of the M1Abrams tanks that guard the Bellagio. He said he thinks there were five tanks total, and unless they got them up and running properly, only one could move. Henry quickly jotted down the locations in his notepad and asked Dunk if there were any other defenses or obstacles they would need to worry about on the way. A flock of pigeons took flight from an alley a few blocks to the east dancing in the sky like a ballet. A moment later three Humvee's accelerated from the alley and skidded onto the Strip. The screech of their run-flat tires echoed off the surrounding casinos. Henry's radio crackled with static and Nella's voice sounded out in an old metallic speaker sound into his ear. She informed him of the Humvee's leaving the alley and that there was no other movement in the vicinity. *Hopefully that's a good thing*, Henry thought.

The sounds of the airport battle were fading and reports of the Federation consolidating their position were coming in over the radio. The constant chatter in his earpiece was equal parts annoying and comforting. He heard Colonel Howard order the vehicles to hold at the airport and he was relieved to hear his voice. It was hard to hear your friends in a battle over the radio. The constant fear that that radio report would be the last thing you would hear them say. Henry's thoughts drifted to Afghanistan and Private Joshua Maxwell and then on to Pennsylvania where they dwelled on Ahmed Elamin and Jonathan Tremblay. *Friends lost in combat.* He was in a daze and barely noticed Frank Simmons swiping at his arm to get his attention. "What is it, Frank?" Henry said, snapping back to the present.

"There's movement on the Bellagio," he said urgently. "Can't make it out through my scope."

Henry adjusted his spotter's scope and focused in on the Bellagio. He quickly scanned the balconies and the Penthouse suite. "Not seen," he said.

"Roof. Looks like three figures," Simmons replied.

"Seen." He adjusted the focus on the scope and there were indeed three figures moving along the roof. He adjusted the zoom to get a better picture and his heart dropped almost to the floor. His hands began to vibrate and he suddenly forgot about the voices chattering in his earpiece. *It can't be*, he thought. He licked the glob of spit that had formed in the corner of his lips and swallowed it with an audible gulp. *It is!* Henry could see them clearly, as though he were standing there with them. He only wished he could hear. Wished he could help. He watched as Commander Lilith Holyfield of the WMA led a chair-bound William Heart being pushed by a large muscular woman towards the edge of the roof. He felt as though he were a ghost. Standing there powerless to help his friend. All he could do was watch. He had forgotten that Simmons, Brynn and Dunk couldn't see until Brynn asked, rather loudly, what was happening. "Holyfield and some muscle-machine of a woman are leading Heart to the edge of the roof," he said.

"What? Why? How?" her questions were frantic. The panic in her voice hung in the air like smoke from one of Simmons' cigarettes.

"I'm not sure. The other woman is pushing him in a chair,"

Henry replied.

"Sofia Hernandez," Dunk said. "She's one of Holyfield's top enforcers. Her and a vicious cunt with purple hair named Sheena Edwards." His voice had a dark note to it.

"They're the ones that fucked me up," Brynn said angrily. She turned to look at Dunk. "What are they doing on the roof?" She could see the sadness grow on his face and she knew she wouldn't like his answer. She asked again. Dunk cleared his throat but didn't speak. Henry said they were tying his hands with rope. Brynn's body vibrated with a terrified nervous energy. She grabbed the scope from Henry and stared through as though she were trying to teleport herself to Heart's location on the roof. "They're standing him on the edge!" she yelled. "Why!"

"It's what she does," Dunk said. "She hangs them over the edge as punishment and a warning."

"Fuck! If I had the .50 cal!" Simmons said through gritted teeth.

Henry moved to press the switch on his radio. Maybe he could have Nella run the rifle up. *We could end this and save...* But it was too late. Time slowed down as they watched Heart fall from the roof. Pushed by Lilith Holyfield. Even from the distance of the Strat, they could all see clearly as Heart plummeted towards the ground, only to be jerked to a stop by the ropes tied to his wrists. The force of the fall whipping him into the tempered glass window caused spider web like cracks to needle their way across the pane. A moment later, his body went limp. Still. As calm as a lake without a ripple of life.

Brynn let out an anguished scream that pierced the war torn city and could have broken windows if she tried. She dropped to her knees with a *thump* and held the scope up limply for Henry to take. Dunk crouched down next to her and placed a tree trunk arm around her shoulders. It was then that the skies ripped open and began to roar like a lion.

CHAPTER 18

October 4th, 2021

Las Vegas, Nevada

Colonel Howard stood in the crew commander's hatch of his IFV, his eyes were level with the roof line like a groundhog peering from its den. He scanned the forward positions of his combat group making mental notes of position and possible vulnerabilities to WMA attacks. For the moment, he had put their combat losses out his mind as he directed the battlefield. The heat from the burning desert sun barely registered on the nape of his neck. Sweat ran down his face from under his helmet. He glanced at his watch, a gift from his section after his final tour in Afghanistan. *Almost time.* He grabbed the talk switch on his radio and depressed the button. His earpiece crackled as he was connected. "Weasel 4 this is 1, you are cleared hot," he said. He let go of the button.

"Weasel 4, roger ETA 1 mike," the voice on the radio responded. Howard smiled. He didn't bother with a reply. *One more minute.*

***

The pilot banked left. Then right. He could see Las Vegas clearly up ahead through the glass canopy of his F16 Fighting Falcon as he leveled the jet. Trailing behind him were two A10 Warthog ground attack planes. Despite his years as a pilot, Major Darnell was nervous as his jet roared through the air towards the city. His heart was pounding as though it were trying to launch itself from his chest like one of the missiles his fighter carried. He had been briefed about the air defense systems in the city. He knew they had them, after all, they shot down six F16's in previous attempts to retake the city. All six of them were his friends. He had been assured that they were destroyed, but couldn't help worry that they missed one, or that there were more that were hidden away. His face wrinkled under his oxygen mask. His greying moustache scraped the inside like a rake on grass.

"Weasel 4 this is 1, you are cleared hot," his earpiece squawked.

"Weasel 4, roger ETA 1 mike," Major Darnell replied. He maneuvered the jet, lining up perfectly with the Strip and began to descend. As the jet screamed through the air, he armed two GBU-39 Small Diameter Bombs and eyed up targets. His first target, the intersection of Tropicana Avenue and Las Vegas Boulevard came into clear view. The jet was low now. It seemed as though it were skimming along the casino rooftops. Closing in on the intersection, Major Darnell thumbed his switch. "Pickle 2," he said into the radio. Pickle, the longtime radio code for a bomb drop. The GBU detached from the F16 with a clunk and soared towards the target. The bomb connected with the asphalt and detonated with a ground shaking explosion that sent debris shooting across the intersection like buckshot. Sandbags burst like balloons filled with fine brown confetti as the explosion tore apart a checkpoint with an 82mm recoilless rifle manned by two soldiers. The rifle tube launched into the air tumbling like an acrobat before landing on the asphalt with a hollow metallic clang. All that remained of its crew looked like something from a John Carpenter movie. Mangled limbs and blood soaked cloth scattered the area.

Major Darnell's F16 thundered past the intersection on his way to the next target. His sights set on the farthest most M1 Abrams from him as he lined up and thumbed the fire switch for a second time. "Pickle 2." The second GBU detached and took off towards the Abrams, gliding effortlessly like an eagle soaring over a national park. It impacted a meter in front of the Abrams, tearing the front of the tank open like a tin can. Bits of shrapnel scattered the area wounding two soldiers and shattering the passenger window of a Humvee, killing the driver. The barrel of the tank bent upwards and split open with a deep metal groan. Fire erupted from the hatches. One less tank. "1 this is Weasel 4, good effect on targets. Over." Major Darnell pulled back hard on the flight control stick and his F16 pitched straight up into the sky. The g-force on his body pressed down on him like he were being crushed by a mountain.

While Major Darnell had been making his attack run, the two A10 Warthogs had moved into position in a line behind him, forming an airborne convoy of death. The smoke from the first GBU explosion that tore apart the sandbagged defensive position was clearing and the pilot of the first A10 angled its nose toward the ground. A line of three Humvee's had been heading down the Strip, weaving around blockades and burnt-out vehicles when the first bomb went off. They stopped quickly and narrowly avoided the impact. The pilot of the A10 set the lead Humvee in his sights and fired. *BRRRRRRRRRRRT.* The gun in the nose of the A10 spit a stream of fire and smoke that launched a long burst of 30mm depleted uranium rounds towards the ground targets. The rounds impacted the Humvee's with such force it tore basketball sized holes in the metal and obliterated the occupants. Smoke and dust kicked up into the air as sparks danced around the impact points. The pilot yanked the flight control stick back and to the right, rolling off into the air. The second A10 pilot was up next. Her sights were set on an M1 Abrams that was positioned near the Bellagio entrance closest to the bombed intersection. She fired. *BRRRRRRRRRRRT.* 30mm depleted uranium rounds slammed into the ground in front of the tank and worked their way across the front fascia, then over the turret, then finally across the back deck that housed the engine. Sparks sprayed into the air from the metal on metal impact. Flames shot out of the engine compartment like a volcano erupting lava. A puff of smoke followed by a jet of flame shot out of the tanks barrel like an angry dragon.

***

Colonel Howard watched with a childlike grin on his face as the three aircraft made their attack runs. The 'brrrt' sound of an A10 was always one of his favourite things. He watched as the F16 dove, bombed, bombed again and then took off high into the sky. He cheered when the first A10 took its turn and his ears sung with that purr of the 30mm gun. His smile grew even wider as the next A10 set up and made its run. *Beautiful.* His earpiece crackled and the pilot of the second A10 spoke excitedly and confidently over the radio. "1 this Wild Beast 2, targets hit. Setting up for another…" Her transmission was cut short. Howard stared down at the radio. Had he accidentally pressed the radio talk switch? No, his hands were up out of the hatch. Maybe someone else cut into the radio traffic by mistake. He was about to shout down into the turret to see if the gunner or driver had been messing around with the switch when the sounds of an explosion finally reached his ears. His heart sank all the way into his abdomen and his jaw dropped almost as far. He looked into the sky to see the second A10 Warthog in flames. It was missing a wing and spiraling towards the ground. It narrowly missed the Stratosphere tower as it descended uncontrollably and tore into a 7-Eleven convenience store ending in a fiery wreck of twisted metal and brick.

"1 this is Weasel 4, they have MANPAD's. I say again. They have MANPAD's!" Major Darnell screamed into the radio. Colonel Howard's eyes darted around scanning for the source of the rocket, an anti-air missile fired from a man-portable air defense system. He could see a faint trail of smoke from the top of the Cosmopolitan Hotel. He pressed his radio talk switch as a second anti-air missile streaked away from the rooftop. It chased Major Darnell's F16 down like a cheetah chasing down a meal on the Serengeti. Darnell deployed chaff, the sparkly counter-measures danced in the air like fireworks. It was no use. The missile was target locked and making its way there fast. Darnell pitched right. The missile followed, closing the gap. He pitched left. The missile adjusted course. Darnell went into a roll. The missile twisted like a corkscrew through the air and detonated on his engine exhaust. The F16 exploded in a flash of red fire and black smoke. The wings jettisoned off to the sides as the smoking remains of the fuselage arced towards the ground in a trail of smoke and flame.

Colonel Howard could hardly breathe. He had no intel to say the WMA had MANPAD's. He ordered Wild Beast 1, the remaining A10, to return to base. He stood in the crew commander's seat, frozen in time. His heart was racing, but he could barely feel it. The blood pounded in his neck like a gorilla beating its chest. He felt a tug on his leg and looked down. His gunner was passing him a lit cigarette. Howard took it with a faint smile and placed it between his dry lips. He hauled on the cigarette until it was almost gone. Like a wakeup call, Howard was ready. He grabbed the switch on his radio and ordered the combat group to press on towards the Las Vegas Strip.

CHAPTER 19

Sheena Edwards lay quietly on the roof of the MGM Grand with the sniper team. The southern-most point of the building offered a perfect view to the airport with clear sightlines for a sniper. Through the spotter's scope she watched the combat group on the airfield stall and not move for a few moments and began to wonder what their plan was. Her mouth was as dry as the desert sand that surrounded the city. The foot soldiers on the airfield were taking cover and she couldn't see any of her soldiers firing at them. She scanned the surroundings, her brain working overtime like an overtaxed engine in a racecar trying to pass a rival. She took a deep breath and pursed her lips. The hairs in her ears resonated as they picked up a roaring sound approaching. Sheena rolled over just as an F16 tore through the air in line with Las Vegas Boulevard. She shielded her eyes with her arm as the jet kicked up dust from the roof top sending particles pirouetting around her like millions of tiny acrobats. Two explosions sounded off like soldiers reporting for duty. Sheena shot to her feet and darted to the opposite edge of the building. She peered over, just in time to see the 82mm recoilless rifle she had placed in position earlier spiraling through the air and landing back on the ground inside a cloud of smoke and dust. She pounded her fist on the edge of the building in anger. A flash of light caught her eye and she cranked her neck to see a column of flame shooting into the air. She couldn't see the source, but knew things were getting bad. She grasped for her radio to call Commander Holyfield when she spotted a second plane approaching. *BRRRRRRRRRRRT.* The sound forced Sheena to her knees as her instincts took over and looked for cover. She trembled as she attempted to peer over the edge of the building, hoping to assess the damage. She caught a glimpse of an A10 Warthog banking off to the north while smoke rose from the street. *BRRRRRRRRRRRT.* A second A10 bolted by spewing smoke and flame and death from its nose. Sheena didn't budge this time. She watched almost in awe as the A10 ascended into the sky. Sparks and smoke went airborne from the street in front of the Bellagio, followed by a second pillar of flame. Sheena's entire body shuddered as a sense of defeat washed over her. She rushed to the stairwell door and took the steps two at a time as she raced to assess the damage on the ground.

***

Lilith Holyfield and Sofia Hernandez stood staring down at William Heart's lifeless body. It hung against the side of the Bellagio like a pennant in an arena. The pair smiled at each other and turned to head inside when a roaring, thundering noise mixed with an explosion like an earsplitting violent cocktail nearly toppled them over the edge. Sofia pulled Lilith from the ledge and attempted to protect her as though she were a child being shielded by a parent. An F16 raced by, rattling the metal guard rails on the roof. Another explosion bellowed out from below as an M1 Abrams was destroyed. Lilith gritted her teeth in anger. Sofia was screaming into her radio for Sheena or anyone that would listen. *BRRRRRRRRRRRT.* The sound of the A10 forced them to cover again. Lilith grabbed the radio from Sofia's large hands and squeezed the talk button hard enough to nearly crack the plastic. "Get those fucking MANPAD's going NOW!" she shrieked into the radio. She watched as the A10 peeled off into the sky. The smoking ruins of the three Humvee's made the desolate road look more apocalyptic if that were possible. *BRRRRRRRRRRRT.* Lilith watched in horror as another M1 Abrams were destroyed as though it were made of tissue paper. The 30mm rounds pierced the armor on the older model tank like a needle piercing fabric. She nearly crushed the radio in her hand. The plastic creaked and groaned as her grip tightened. The A10 was soaring higher when a streak of smoke launched from the roof of the Cosmopolitan Hotel and chased the A10 down, the missile detonating next to its left wing in a flash of flame and a puff of black-white smoke. She smiled a satisfied grin as she watched it spiral out of control narrowly hitting the Stratosphere tower and erupting in flame in the distance. She smiled and told Sofia to get Sheena on the radio and they headed inside. Another missile was let loose from the Cosmopolitan as soon as they closed the door.

***

Henry, Brynn, Simmons and Dunk all cheered as the F16 soared past the Stratosphere tower. It had been years since they had proper air support on a mission and the sight made them feel giddy like school children. Henry, Simmons and Dunk were all thinking back to the times they had air support in the Middle East and how comforting it was. Especially against an enemy with no air defense. Henry and Simmons assessed the damage through their scopes while Brynn and Dunk continued to cheer. The dust and smoke near the Bellagio was a good sign they all thought. Less to deal with later. Their smiles grew wider when they noticed the A10's lining up for a gun-run. *BRRRRRRRR-RRRT.* The first A10 blasted the three Humvee's that had left the alley near them a little while ago. Henry shuddered at the thought of seeing the inside of the vehicles. If there was any-thing left of the inside. Brynn jumped up and down as the A10 banked past the tower. The heat trails from the twin-turbofan engines blurred the blue sky behind them. Dunk gave a salute.

Aaron radioed up to say it was one hell of a fucking surprise and that Nella nearly shit her pants. The four at the top of the tower were laughing when an M1 Abrams in front of the Bellagio ruptured into sparks and flames. *BRRRRRRRRRRRT.* The fun thing about the A10 is unless you're near the impact zone, you usually see the impacts before you hear the gun.

The A10 was headed towards them and beginning to ascend into the sky when one of the wings blew off in a violent bang. The plane spiraled towards them. They dove for cover, for all the good that would do them, and braced for impact. The plane skimmed the edge of the tower showering them in sparks and bits of metal. The heat from the engines and fire where the wing should be singed the hairs on their necks. Seconds later, they heard the explosion from behind the tower. Simmons was the first up and ran to the other side to see the damage. He radioed for Colonel Howard but received only static in reply. He jaunted back to the others just as another missile was streaking towards the F16. Their hearts raced. They watched the jet bank. They braced. The missile corrected. The jet banked again. They clenched their teeth. The missile adjusted. The chaff counter measures deployed. They felt relief that turned to heartache when the missile collided with the jet in mid spiral. They watched in horror as the wings separated and the fuselage hurried to the ground. Debris shot out into the air from the crash site. They stood silently for a moment as the surviving A10 flew out of sight. Then Henry solemnly said "C'mon, let's move."

CHAPTER 20

October 4th, 2021

Las Vegas, Nevada

Nella placed her hand on Brynn's shoulder. "You okay?" She asked sympathetically. Brynn nodded and smiled a weak little smile before moving out towards the street. Smoke blew on the wind from the downed A10 passing them like a pedestrian in traffic. An eerie quiet washed over the Strip like a slow rising tide. Aaron paced back and forth amongst the debris strewn about the towers entrance like a tiger stuck in a cage. His fists clenched in tight balls. His face was as red as the hairs in his beard. Aaron and Nella hadn't seen what happened to William Heart, but that didn't make them any less furious. When Henry had told them what happened, Nella dropped to her knees, her heart broke and her hands trembled. It took every ounce of strength Aaron had not to rush headfirst and take on the WMA alone. His body vibrated with an energy that could power a freight train. That energy burst through him like a dam exploding as he rushed at Dunk, pinning him to the wall. Their muscular forms pressed against one another creating a hulking mass. Dunk raised his hands as though he said he surrendered.

"You fucking knew!" Aaron screamed. "Didn't you!" Tendrils of spit flew from his mouth.

"I knew she did this, but not that she was going to do it to Heart," Dunk said calmly. Simmons and Henry rushed over and each grabbed a shoulder of Aaron's husky width. They attempted to pull him back but his feet were firmly planted like the roots of a giant redwood tree. He pushed Dunk further into the wall like he was trying to press him into the concrete and through to the other side. Dunk kept his hands raised. His face was stoic in expression. He needed Aaron to see that he was on his side. Simmons and Henry tugged harder on Aaron's shoulders and pleaded with him to *just fucking stop*.

"Let's just fucking move," Aaron said gruffly. He released

his grip on Dunk and shook his shoulders free of the hands that grasped them. He swung his M249 around from his hip and followed Brynn out to the street. Henry patted Dunk on the arm and asked if he was good. Dunk nodded but didn't say anything in reply. He shook the tension from his arms and headed towards the street.

***

Henry moved in behind an abandoned sandbagged checkpoint in the middle if the street. Dust kicked up into the air as he crouched down for cover while Simmons maintained watch through the scope of his M14. He had two-person fire teams on each flank. Aaron and Brynn moved along the south side of the street in a low crouch as though they were ducking under invisible wires. Nella and Dunk moved along the sidewalk on the north side, scanning the casinos for movement. Eruptions of gunfire and the detonation of explosions echoed off from the east as the combat group had resumed its battle. Henry pulled his canteen from the side pouch of his chest rig and took a swig. The mouthful of water was still cool despite the desert heat. "How the fuck does a CIA Agent flip like this?" he asked no one in particular. Simmons shrugged in response. "It had to be money, right? But like... still." Henry tapped the canteen in Simmons bicep. The water sloshed around inside. Simmons shook his head. Henry returned the canteen to its pouch and snapped the plastic buckle closed with a *click*.

The fire teams on his flanks pushed close to twenty meters further and held position. The pace was slow moving as they snaked their way towards the Bellagio. The distraction had paid off like a lottery win as most of the city's defenses had been repositioned to the east. And, despite the unfortunate loss of two planes, their attack runs had caused significant damage and morale loss. While they were making their way down the long staircase of the Stratosphere, the radio had been squawking off reports of WMA soldiers surrendering and a small group of deserters fleeing the city to the south. Henry got up onto one knee and swung his G36-C over the sandbags. He scanned for movement quickly and then vaulted over the sandbags, knocking one to the ground with his boot. Simmons snickered as he followed Henry in a more graceful way. They had barely moved five meters from their sandbagged cover when a burst of machine gun fire cut across their path. The rounds impacted the asphalt in front of them sending them diving for cover behind a concrete road divider. Chips of concrete and dust sprayed over them like a thick mist as the machine gunner zeroed in on their position. *Crack Crack Crack!* Henry and Simmons hunkered down. *Crack Crack Crack!*

Aaron shouldered his M249, flipping off the safety as he swung the weapon up. His cheek pressed against the stock as his scraggly red beard hairs crinkled and wrapped around the metal. Puffs of smoke and sparks sprang out from the front window of a dilapidated CVS Pharmacy across the street as more rounds flew through the air and thumped into the concrete barrier that was shielding Henry and Simmons. Aaron squeezed the trigger and the bolt of the machine gun clunked forward firing off an extended burst into the CVS. The soldiers in the pharmacy turned their attention to Aaron and Brynn who dove for cover behind a tipped over postal truck as rounds cracked around them, sparking off the metal of the truck.

Nella and Dunk pushed forward down the street on the north side and set up a position across the intersection from the pharmacy. Nella fired four single shots into the pharmacy from her M4. She heard a scream ring out that pierced the air like a dart. *Crack Crack Crack!* The machine gun switched targets sending a volley of copper-jacketed lead in their direction. She could see Henry peering around the side of the barrier from her position and shot him a thumbs up.

Henry stole himself back into cover and gave Simmons a thumbs up who nodded in acknowledgment. The gunfire from the CVS had increased in volume and intensity. *More fighters are joining in.* Three single shots rang out to their south as Brynn fired on their attackers. Henry and Simmons quickly, in unison, rose to their knee and swung their weapons over the barrier. The machine gunner was now firing at Brynn and Aaron's position. Henry fired three quick shots into the open window. The recoil of his rifle sent each shot a little higher than the last but that was fine, he needed to give Simmons time. Like a rehearsed play, Simmons had lined up his sight on the machine gunner and fired a single shot. The machine gunner's hat jumped into the air as he slumped to the ground taking the gun with him. Rounds tore through the tall glass window as his lifeless finger tightened around the trigger. Fighters in the building, *there must have been at least two more*, turned their fire towards Henry and Simmons who ducked back into cover. *Crack Crack Crack Crack Crack Crack!*

The uncontrolled rapid fire of a soldier who was beginning to panic.

Nella and Dunk pressed up to the CVS as rounds zipped and cracked by like tiny supersonic jets. Sparks burst out from the shattered glass windows. *They were close*, Nella thought. She pointed to the sparks and Dunk nodded. A second later the gunfire stopped and they could hear the hollow metal of an empty magazine scrapping along the magazine housing of a rifle. The spring inside the magazine rattled against the aluminum as it hit the tile flooring. Dunk sprinted in through the open doors first, catching the soldier by surprise. Dunk fired his KRISS Vector at the soldier delivering a rapid burst of fifteen .45ACP rounds to the soldier's chest throat and face. Wisps of pink and red swirled in the air as the bullets tore through him. He slumped on the ground in a gory heap as blood jetted out from his severed carotid artery. Nella had followed Dunk in like she were a car in a train, detaching as she cleared the door frame and swept in to the left of the pharmacy. A soldier cracked off a single shot from behind the cash register that whizzed between Nella and Dunk. Nella's M4 was at the ready and before she had time to think, her muscle memory had taken the wheel. The sight on her M4 lined up on the assailants upper torso. Her finger pulled on the trigger. She could feel the click as the sear disengaged and released the hammer into the firing pin. The 5.56mm round tore through the air and perforated the soldier's skin like a paper target on a range. He collapsed to the floor and gurgled as his throat filled with blood. By the time Nella had glided her way across the pharmacy, the soldier lay dead, still clutching his bloody gullet.

***

"Alright," Henry whispered, "There's the one remaining tank that stands in our way." He pointed towards the Bellagio. They had taken cover on the deck of a pedestrian overpass to get eyes on their objective. The remains of a burning M1 Abrams sitting in the intersection filled the air with smoke that clouded their view. Past that however was another Abrams positioned on a platform that had been constructed in the center of the Bellagio Fountain like a stage at a concert. The tank was surrounded with a thick smattering of sandbags that hid the sides and front from anti-tank weapons. The turret scanned back and forth slowly. The crew were on high alert as the combat group inched closer from the east.

A massive explosion sounded off like a giants roar and a spiral of smoke billowed into the air. The tank briefly turned its attention east towards the explosion, and then resumed scanning the Strip. Henry suggested moving south and flanking the tank. Aaron nodded in agreement, but Simmons disagreed. "We should avoid it, push in around back of the building." He said.

"We have to take that tank out," Aaron retorted, "or it'll fuck whoever comes around the corner."

"I'm with Frank. If we stop Holyfield, we end this," Brynn interjected.

"Fuck it," Henry said, "We're doing both." Brynn opened her mouth to speak but Henry held a hand up to stop her. "Aaron and I will flank around behind the tank and pop its top with a frag. Dunk, I need you to get Nella, Brynn and Frank into the Bellagio and start sweeping for Holyfield. We'll link up when we're done. Hoorah?"

"Hoorah!" they said in unison.

The team of four set off towards the rear of the Bellagio while Aaron and Henry crept slowly towards the front. They made their way across the street and snaked through the mall that wrapped around the fountain. They encountered no resistance which was a blessing, but also terrifying at the same time. Henry couldn't help but choke back a gob of phlegm at the thought of a hundred soldiers waiting for them by the tank. He pushed the thought aside and slowly creaked open a door to a restaurant patio. The door groaned like it were hanging in an old Victorian style haunted house. Henry stopped it when he was sure they both could fit through and moved towards the railing. The tank platform was no more than fifty meters away, *a quick jaunt and it's done.* Henry balled his fist and pretended to pull a pin from it. Aaron nodded and slung his M249 across his back. They each pulled an M67 fragmentation grenade from their pouches and hopped the railing. They sprinted across the platform bridge as though they were running the 100m dash in the Summer Olympics. They hopped up onto the back of the tank. Their boots thudded on the metal in a muted rubber-me-tallic clang. The gunner's hatch swung open and a voice said "You're not supposed to relieve us for another twenty minutes!" The gunner stood up on his seat and swung his body around to come face to face with Aaron Walsh.

Aaron smiled through his wiry beard and without hesita-tion, decked the gunner in the teeth cracking them in the process.

He pulled the pin on his grenade. Henry did the same. Together, they tossed the grenades into the hatch and shut the lid. They sprinted back to the patio and just made it over the railing when the grenades detonated. The turret launched into the air, fifty or maybe sixty feet. Henry wasn't sure but it slammed down into the dry fountain bed with a force that suggested that it fell from space. Flame and smoke spewed from the body of the tank. Henry and Aaron collected themselves and vacated the area before WMA soldiers came to investigate. At the top of the Bellagio, William Heart's body swayed in the gentle breeze.

CHAPTER 21

October 4th, 2021

Las Vegas, Nevada

Colonel Howard sat pressed up against a waist high sandbag wall. He clutched his side trying to put pressure on the gaping wound that was spilling his blood like a faucet. The charred carcass of his IFV sat in the intersection. A burning body of one of the crew hung over the edge. The gunner, the one who passed him the cigarette, *Reid Brown. A good kid. Fuck.* He stared for a moment, the flames flickered off the soldiers back as though he were a log in a fireplace. Dust puffed up into the air, jerking the flames around as rounds peppered his body. The last half hour had been a blur. The combat group pushed into the Strip and managed to sweep through the intersection of Las Vegas Boulevard and Tropicana Avenue with ease. The air attacks had caused the WMA defenses to falter at first but the remaining soldiers were quick to regroup and counter attack. He was caught by surprise when an M1 Abrams rounded a corner at their rear and managed to take out four Federation Abrams and three more IFV's, including his before being destroyed by a Javelin missile.

He was replaying the scenario in his head over and over again as he pressed a bloody wad of gauze into his wound. He had ordered the move forward and they had come under fire from a roof top. *What happened next?* Two of the lead tanks had pushed around the corner and were making their way towards the Bellagio. *Then what?* They were knocked out by RPG fire from the surrounding buildings. *Not good. What next?* We rounded the corner behind another tank and engaged the RPG teams.

He looked down at the gauze that had been completely soaked through, dying it a deep crimson colour. He tossed it aside. It made a sickening wet slap when it hit the ground, like a t-shirt wet from the rain. *Fucking useless. What happened after?* He had ordered dismounted soldiers to sweep through the buildings. They made quick work of the WMA soldiers. Glass rained down on the vehicles as bullets soared from building to building, shredding the windows and the soldiers alike. *We took losses, right?* Howard tried to calculate the combats groups' losses. There were the four tanks on the airfield with an APC, plus the one with the engine failure they left behind. Two more IFV's bought the farm before the airport had been secured. *What else?* There was the F16 and an A10. *Is that all?* Howard furrowed his brow, closed his eyes and thought hard. He could see the two lead tanks destroyed, and the four in the rear. *That's ten tanks!* He could see the three IFV's burning. *So much loss! Do you have enough? Retreat? Push on? Give up?* His thoughts were racing like cars on a slot track, zipping around at a high rate of speed always close to shooting off the track. *What about the purple-haired wom-an?*

His eyes shot open. He had forgotten about the pur-ple-haired woman. He recalled seeing her directing troops. She was skillful in her deployments. He remembered being amazed at her ferocity and tenacity in the face of a stronger force. *A stronger force. There's a fucking joke!* He remembered making eye contact with her moments before the tank engaged his IFV.

Their eyes locked in a dance. Sizing each other up like two lions about to fight for control of the pride. She had smiled a vicious, evil looking smile before the explosion tore through his abdomen. He coughed a spray of blood that misted the air in front of him. "Where is she?" he thought.

"Right here," a woman's voice said playfully behind him.

You idiot, you said that shit out loud! "Wh…Who?" he stammered.

Sheena hopped off the front of a disabled APC. Its occupants were strewn about the intersection in bloody heaps. She walked around to the front of Howard, giving him a wide berth like a wolf circling its prey. The evil looking smile was painted on her face like a beautiful villain. "You almost had us there," she said, looking down at her feet. "But," she motioned to the destruction around her, "We didn't do too bad." She walked towards him and crouched down in front of him. His skin was pale and clammy looking, like he had the worst fever he's ever had. He reached out to grab her but the strength left his body. His arm flopped down to the side.

"Wh…Who?" he asked again. His voice was as weak as his arm.

"Yeah, we're pretty much done here now though," she said, looking around. "Your last guys and tanks are descending on the Bellagio now. Radio told me there's been fighting inside for almost a half hour. Did you have another force attack from the west? Sneaky Sneaky. Anyway, I think I'll cut and run now." She smiled her evil smile. Her left hand pulled on the Colt 1911 and withdrew it from its holster. She toggled the safety and pressed the cool metal barrel to Howard's head. "Name's Shee-na." *BANG!*

CHAPTER 22

October 4th, 2021

Las Vegas, Nevada

Dunk and Brynn took cover behind a concrete pillar, pressed against it like they were walking a narrow ledge. A grenade scattered shrapnel around the room sending bits of slot machine and chair fabric twirling through the air as the jagged metal grenade shards ripped apart the old casino amenities. Nella and Simmons laid down suppressing fire. The report of their guns echoing throughout the gaming floor. Henry and Aaron sprinted as they flanked around two soldiers who were preparing another grenade from behind an old roulette table that lay on its side like a decaying farm animal. Aaron cut them down a burst from his M249 SAW. He quickly scooped up the grenade, pulled the pin and chucked it like a baseball towards the cash office, where four soldiers had taken up position. The blast sent poker chips and bills of American cash airborne. "That's one way to do it," Henry said through a smile. Aaron grinned and moved to peer into the office. The smoke left a lingering scent of death, destruction and explosive in the air.

Dunk pushed passed them and scanned the next casino room for movement. "We have to move," he said "if shit's going south for Lilith, she'll either burn the building down or bail." He pushed into the next room with his Vector shouldered, ready to fire at any target that pops up. The lights were flickering with each explosion that sounded off from outside. The air was stale, like a layer of dust had been kicked up all at once. They fought back sneezes as they moved forward.

Henry's earpiece crackled with life as a soldier that goes by call sign One-One-Alpha stated that they had breached the front entrance of the Bellagio. *Howard's rocking it*, he thought. They pushed forward to an elevator bank and started pressing the up buttons. The power flickered again and they all glanced around nervously. Simmons suggested the stairs and received no argument in response. Henry split them into two fire teams. Nella, Aaron and Simmons would take the west stairs to the roof level while he, Brynn and Dunk took the east stairs to the Penthouse level. A quick fist bump like athletes before a game and they were off.

***

They panted heavily as they climbed. The air was hot and musty in the stairwell. Like it had never seen a breeze before. Sweat poured down their backs sticking their shirts to them as though they were made of tape. Simmons swore more than a drunken sailor during the climb and more than once said he hopes Lilith Holyfield was on the roof so he could shoot her in the fucking face for making him climb all these stairs. Nella reminded him more than once that the stairs were his idea. Aaron had been falling back a bit, but under the guise of needing to check something. They finally reached the roof level and took a moment to slow their heart rates and compose themselves before they burst through the doors. After a quick agreement that they were ready, Simmons kicked the door open and spun out of the way. Nella swung into the doorway, then moved left.

Aaron swung in and moved right. Four WMA soldiers by the ledge whirled around and sprinted for cover as Nella and Aaron opened fire. Simmons pinned himself to the wall like a poster in a bedroom as rounds cracked through the open door. Nella took cover behind an air conditioning unit as she reloaded her M4. The magazine slid into place with a click and she smacked the bolt catch with her left hand. Aaron heard Nella resume firing and ducked down behind some ventilation shafts to change the box on his M249. Simmons leaned back awkwardly and fired two rounds towards the soldiers, sending them into cover. He took that moment to move and sprinted through the door. Dust plumed up from the force of his boots on the roof as they propelled him into cover next to Aaron. One of the soldiers let out a scream as a 5.56mm round from Nella ripped through his shoulder in a spray of blood and a wisp of dust. The soldier spun and took cover. The one to his left moved to try and flank, but Aaron saw his movement in his peripheral. He spun his M249 and cut the soldier down with a burst. The soldier dropped and slid on the roof for a half a foot before slumping over on his side. Rounds cracked around Aaron sending him back into cover. Simmons stayed low and worked his way around the ventilation shafts and got an angle on another soldier. She was firing at Nella who was pinned behind her air condition-er. Sparks sprayed through the air like fireworks as the bullets pelted the metal unit. Simmons fired two shots dropping the soldier in her place.

The final soldier screamed for them to wait and stuck his hands up over his cover. He and the wounded soldier stood up slowly. Nella stepped out of cover as a single shot rang out. Simmons dropped the wounded soldier who was raising his rifle in his good arm. Nella took a breath and nodded at Simmons. He nodded back. The surrendering soldier stood still with his arms up. He was practically a statue except for the shake in his legs and the urine running down into his boots. "You guys secure him," Aaron said, "I've got William." He walked to the edge of the building and began to pull the body of William Heart back to the roof.

***

Henry and Dunk were pinned on one side of the hallway in a smaller suite while Brynn was pinned in one on the other side. The suites were matching and offered different views but were well appointed and obviously lived in. There were men's clothes and extra pieces of weaponry laid out. Dunk said they were the quarters for Lilith's personal guards. Chunks of drywall were sent flying through the hall leading to the Penthouse as rounds slammed into the walls. It seemed strange to Henry that no one was covering the door to the stairwell, it would have been an easy kill box. He figured panic was setting in as the WMA was being decimated. Panic had a way of making tactics falter. They had been allowed to stroll into the hallway like regular patrons of the hotel and make their way towards the Penthouse Suite before they were fired upon. Rounds continued to chip away at the wooden door frames. Splinters hopped through the air like tiny strings of confetti. Henry held his rifle around the corner and blindly fired a quick burst of automatic fire, sending the two guards into cover.

The sounds of a suppressed sub-machine gun announcing itself resonated through the hallway as 9mm rounds crashed into the wall in front of Henry and Dunk's door. Henry pulled his rifle back into the room. *Mother-fucker!* Blood ran down his arm as the pain from a round grazing his right bicep radiated up his shoulder and into his head. His heart pounded as though it were trying to push every ounce of blood and plasma through the new hole in his body. Dunk asked if he was good. Henry told him he was, but shit was turning to fuck fast and they needed to do something.

Brynn's C8 fired a burst of 5.56 into the hallway. "That's my gun you fucking bitch!" she screamed as she reloaded. Sofia Hernandez peered from the doorway of the Penthouse with a smile and fired another burst from Brynn's suppressed MP5.

"Come and fucking get it!" she yelled back over the gun-fire. She motioned for the two guards to move up with her left hand as she swung the MP5 from side to side scanning for move-ment.

The two male guards crept forward stepping purposefully as they moved. Sofia ducked back into the room and pulled a fresh magazine from Brynn's former chest rig. She tossed the empty magazine from the housing on the MP5 and slid the fresh one in. It clicked in place with metallic *click* and she slapped the bolt handle forward out of its locked back position. She was ready to go.

Brynn's eyes darted around the room as she scanned for anything that could help them out. A pile of neatly folded black t-shirts sat on the top of the dresser waiting for their owner to put them away. Next to them were a single pair of tan cargo pants, folded just as neat. *Useless.* The kitchenette was small and the counter was a black stone like material of either quartz or granite. Brynn couldn't tell. Two water bottles stood gracefully next to a black belt with some olive green cylindrical objects attached. She dashed over to the counter and snatched the belt that held three Nine-Banger concussion grenades. A smile spread over her face as she pulled one of the Nine-Banger's from its black fabric holder. She moved to the open door waving the Nine-Banger from side-to-side to show Henry and Dunk. Henry was wrapping some gauze around his arm and mouthed the word 'yes'. Dunk mimicked Brynn's smile and moved towards his suites door. Brynn pulled the pin, holding the grenade tightly in her left hand, and gave Dunk a nod that said *ready*.

The two guards were closing in on the suite doors when Dunk stuck his Vector out and fired an un-aimed burst of .45ACP into the hallway. The two guards dove for cover behind some planters that lined the hall and Sofia ducked back into the Penthouse suite. Brynn chucked the Nine-Banger into the hall and within two seconds the grenade detonated into nine consecutive flashes and bangs that filled the hall with bright lights, deafening booms and smoke like a small venue rock concert. Without hesitation, Brynn and Dunk peeled out of their rooms and pushed forward down the hall. The smoke swirled behind them as they moved. The two guards were on the ground coughing and rubbing their eyes. Brynn fired a single shot into the T-box of the one on the right side. He went flaccid like one of those wooden toys you press the bottom of and they fall over. The other guard staggered to his feet with a SCAR-L in his hands. He let out a cough as he tried to shoulder the rifle. The long burst from Dunk's Vector tipped him backwards as a pray of blood misted the hallway behind him. Henry had pushed out of the room after tightening the gauze on his arm and was moving in the center of the hallway covering the door to the Penthouse. Brynn tossed another Nine-Banger into the suite and they pushed in as soon as it fired off its last *bang*.

The three of them moved into the main living room of the suite. The white marble floor was stained with black marks and blood. Chips of marble, wood and drywall lay strewn about the floor from the bullets that had recently torn through the room. Smoke churned about the room as they pushed in and swept clear the main living area.

Brynn moved towards the kitchen and dining area. The ornate decoration stood in contrast to the derelict remains of the rest of the city. Gold trims accentuated the grandeur of the suite and a crystal chandelier stood pointedly above the glossy black dining table. The area was clear and Brynn pressed towards the kitchen. The green handguards of her C8 creaked as her nervous grip tightened on the Sure Fire forward grip. She moved through the open kitchen door and was struck in the rifle by a metal serving tray. The force of the blow shoved her arms down causing her finger to squeeze the trigger. A single shot fired into the tile floor and ricocheted up into the oven, shattering the glass. Sofia swung the tray again, this time at Brynn's face. Brynn dodged the attack and swung her rifle up. Before she could get a proper aim, Sofia dropped the tray and tackled Brynn to the cold tile.

***

Henry and Dunk moved towards the bedrooms. There were two, a master bedroom that stood at the end of the hall and a smaller bedroom on the left. The small bedroom was still bigger than most bedrooms Henry had ever seen. The large king sized bed sat positioned against the wall so you could see a stunning view of the city. They swept through and cleared the room. Finding nothing, they pushed to the next room. The door was shut so Henry forcefully kicked it open sending wood splinters and dust into the room. Dunk pushed into the room rapidly. Before Henry could follow him in, a blast from a shotgun sprayed smoke and fire towards them as a 12 gauge slug shredded Dunk's prosthetic leg. He fell to the floor with a thud that Henry could feel through the tile as he fired his Vector at Lilith Holyfield, sending her diving into cover behind a large desk. Henry could hear the action of the pump shotgun work as Lilith chambered another slug, the spent shell ejected and bounced playfully on the marble floor. Henry sprinted into the room letting loose a volley of automatic fire pinning Lilith in place behind her desk. He fired as he ran, stooping to grab Dunk by the vest and pull him into cover behind a half wall that separated the bedroom and en suite bathroom.

***

Sofia pressed her palms firmly into Brynn's throat as she

squeezed. Bubbles of spit burst from her lips as Brynn coughed and gasped for air. Sofia's tanned skin turned a cherry red as she tensed her whole body. Brynn's arms twisted wildly on the floor until her fingers felt the cold metal ridge of the serving tray. She grasped it tightly and swung her arm up with all her strength driving the tray into the side of Sofia's nose. Blood rained down onto Brynn as Sofia released her throat and stumbled backwards. Her nose was broken, again, and bent sideways like a warped piece of clay. Blood gushed down the front of her chest rig. Her eyes welled with tears. "You fucking bitch!" she screamed. "My d'ose!" Her hands kept attempting to straighten the nose, but the pain caused them to jerk away.

Brynn rolled onto her side as she sucked back deep breaths of air. Her throat felt like it had been trampled by an elephant. She pushed herself to her feet. Shaking, she turned to face Sofia. "My…fucking…turn…" her voice was raspy as she wheezed out the words. She clenched her fists and threw a punch, connecting her right fist to the side of Sofia's jaw. She followed up with a left. Sofia's head rocked back and forth as Brynn's fists landed their attacks. Sofia staggered backwards and swiped her arms across the metal stone countertop sending a container of cooking utensils and basket of fruit flying towards Brynn.

Sofia counter attacked with a swing from her hulking right arm. Her fist skimmed Brynn's shoulder as her watery eyes blurred her vision. Brynn stepped forward to throw another punch but Sofia grabbed her and squeezed her in a bear hug like a wrestler in a cage match. She threw Brynn onto the counter and made a grab for her throat again. Brynn cocked her leg back and hurtled her boot into Sofia's gut, sending her to the floor gasping for air and holding back vomit.

Brynn moved quickly off the counter and rushed to her rifle that had slid along the floor to the dining area. Her fingers clutched it just as she was tackled from behind. They tumbled into the dining room and Sofia grabbed the back of Brynn's vest, raising her up off her feet. She tossed Brynn onto the black glossy table and wiped blood and spit away from her mouth. Sofia jerked her arms as though she were resetting them and moved towards the table. Brynn rolled over with a smile on her face. Her rifle aimed perfectly at Sofia. "This is for William," she said sorrowfully. The rifle recoiled in her arms as a round burst out from the barrel and struck Sofia in her already broken nose. She heaped to the floor in a pool of blood. Brynn relaxed and wheezed a long breath.

***

Marble tile scattered across the room as Lilith blasted the half wall with slugs. The thumb-sized hunks of lead punched through the wall forcing Henry and Dunk to adjust themselves behind the cover. "You think you can just off me!" she yelled. "This is *my* fucking city!" She pumped the slide on her shotgun and fired another shot. The slug skimmed over Henry's shoulder as bits of stone scraped along his cheek.

"It's over Lilith," Dunk shouted "It's been over for a while. Just give up and we'll take you in." Another slug pierced the wall. Their ears were ringing a high pitch squeal.

"Commander Holyfield," Henry said, "Let us take you in. The Federation will put you up in a nice cell. Three hot meals a day…"

"You think *I* fucking care about that! I worked hard for *years* to build this alliance and the Federation just rolls in and destroys it. Destroys all I built. Kills my fucking son!"

"All that you built?" Dunk asked, "Lilith, people are starving. The only people fed well are your personal lackeys. It's a god damned joke!"

"Brave words from a fucking traitor," Lilith said through clenched teeth. The wall had been blasted to pieces and offered no more cover than a cardboard box. It was nothing short of a miracle that they hadn't been hit yet. Lilith told them to come out and she'll make their deaths easy on them.

Dunk stuck his hands up first, then struggled to stand up on one leg. His metal prosthetic leg hung from one undamaged hinge. Henry stood next. His arms not as high as dunks. She motioned with the barrel of the shotgun to move and head towards the balcony. They shuffled slowly as Dunk hobbled on his good leg. Frustrated and tired, Lilith jabbed the barrel of the shotgun into Dunk's back, sending him sprawling out on the Penthouse balcony. Henry turned and lunged for the weapon. He caught Lilith of guard. The look of surprise on her face was like a mask made of fear. Henry pulled on the gun as he drove his boot into her thigh, forcing her off balance. She relaxed her grip enough for Henry to free the gun from her hands but before he could swing it around on her, she drove her shoulder into his gut. The shotgun tumbled into the suite as Henry hunched over for breath. Lilith swung her leg around in a roundhouse kick to Henry's jaw splitting his lip and leaving him sprawled out on the ground. "Now," she said brushing a tendril of hair from her face, "where were we?" She reached to her side for the shotgun that is usually slung there, briefly forgetting Henry had wrangled it free. She took a deep breath and turned around to head into the suite.

The back of her chest rig exploded in an outburst of tan fabric, ceramic plating and a mist of pinkish-red blood. She stumbled. Her face frozen in shock. Brynn Parker stood in the balcony doorway and pumped the action on the shotgun. Smoke flowed from the barrel. Lilith attempted to take another step forward but the second shot to her chest propelled her backwards and over the balcony railing. Brynn walked forward and peered over the railing. She stared for a moment then spat a large wad of spit to the ground below. She turned around with a smile and helped Henry and Dunk to their feet. It was finally over.

CHAPTER 23

October 30th, 2021

Las Vegas, Nevada

Henry Carson, Nella Saba, Frank Simmons, Aaron Walsh, Brynn Parker and James 'Dunk' Turner all stood at attention next to the two caskets draped in Canadian Flags. The trumpeter began to play Last Post as the caskets were lowered into the grave site outside of Area 51. Soldiers slid the flags off the caskets and folded them into a neatly pointed triangle before handing one to Henry and one to Brynn. One Four Delta saluted their fallen comrades, William Heart and James Howard who were among the casualties of the Battle for Las Vegas. Henry had had the privilege of working with both men for years and could not have been more proud to call them his friends.   The ceremony ended with a twenty-one gun salute that made every single person in attendance flinch. An effect that would last for years.

As the sun set, One Four Delta sat in their tent lines with an old bottle of whiskey they pulled from Colonel James Howard's reserved stash and poured a glass for each of them. Henry then poured a glass for William and James, setting them on his barracks box. They all raised their glasses and solemnly said, *We knew them. We will remember them and they will not be forgotten.* Sitting quietly, they sipped their whiskey.

***

It took some time to get used to being called Colonel, but Henry was settling nicely into the role. His first order of business was to promote Brynn to Major and turn his command of One Four Delta over to her. It took some convincing, but Henry was sure that she was right for the job. Her only condition was that he make Dunk a permanent member of the team to which Henry happily obliged. He called the team to the Command Centre for a small ceremony where he granted Dunk the rank of Lieutenant. Dunk stood proudly at attention. His large figure dwarfed Henry as he placed the Lieutenant insignia on his uniform. Henry took a step back and they saluted each other. As Henry moved to face Brynn, Dunk stood at ease and the hydraulics in his new leg let out a hiss. Simmons let out a quiet snicker. Brynn came to attention and fought back a tear as Henry placed the Major insignia on her uniform. Her thoughts swirled in a ball of happiness, sadness, gratitude and remorse. Henry read the look on her face and smiled lightly, nodding at her. He took a step back as they saluted each other.

Major Parker and Colonel Carson walked from the command tent back to the SOFREC lines amid the setting sun. The sky on the horizon was a pleasant orange like a water colour painting. As they walked they discussed needed equipment, gear, weapons and a replacement for Henry's position. Henry nodded along in agreement. *She's got this.* Henry suggested that she speak to the team before submitting a requisition and that his biggest piece of advice was to never discount their opinions. "You'll make mistakes, hell, I did. But they will always have your back. No matter what." Henry shook her hand and congratulated her again. Brynn took a step back, saluted and then ducked into the tent. Henry nodded at the tent lines as he could hear One Four

Delta laughing. In the background his old iPod he gifted them

played a song of memories. A smile spread across his face as he

headed back to the Command Center.

EPILOGUE

February 9th, 2022

Calgary, Alberta

The thermometer read -25°C but it had to be colder than that. Dunk was pretty sure he would freeze instantly if he took his parka off. *Fuckin' bullshit!* His toes were starting to go numb as he stood in the air sentry hatch at the back of One Four Delta's LAV III. The eight wheeled vehicle cut through the snow like a knife as it moved along Highway 2 towards High River, Alberta. Someone tapped Dunk on the leg and the metal let out a ping sound that Dunk couldn't hear over the roar of the LAV's caterpillar engine. He felt the tap on his other leg and looked down to see a steaming hot Styrofoam cup of coffee being held out by Frank Simmons. "Thanks, Brother," he said over a smile as he grabbed the cup and sat down. "This winter shit is fucking horse-shit," he said, "How do people even live here?" He sipped the coffee and felt the warmth radiate through his body like an internal heater.

"You get used to it," Simmons said, pulling a scarf over his face and taking Dunk's spot in the air sentry hatch.

"I'll never get used to it."

"Major Parker, mam," a voice cracked over the vehicles internal radio, "the convoy is slowing down."

"Roger, Emma," Brynn replied, "and you can call me Brynn you know."

"You'll catch on quick, kid," Aaron said from the gunner's seat. The convoy slowed to a halt and vehicles began to spread out in a circle to create a defensive position. Brynn pulled herself up onto the roof of the LAV and told Emma to follow her and Nella. The snow sprang up into a low level cloud under her boots as she jumped down from the LAV.

The three walked slowly towards a small group of four vehicles positioned in the center of the circular defensive position. Colonel Carson was sitting on the bench in the back of a

LAV with its ramp down. He sipped a coffee while studying a map. Soldiers around the defensive position were refilling vehicles from jerry cans of diesel. The smell filled the air like an old gas station. Brynn nodded at Henry as she stopped at the bottom of the ramp. She placed her right foot on the ramp and leaned forward slightly. Her hands were tucked in behind her chest rig for warmth. "This is Emma Wolfe, newest member of One Four Delta," she said. Henry looked up from his map and smiled.

"Sir," Emma said nervously.

"Welcome aboard, Wolfe," he said, "you ready for this?" he asked.

"Absolutely sir. Do you have a plan?"

"Think she's still in Calgary?" Brynn asked.

"If the intel is correct, she's here. She's got the city well defended and we're going to take her out," Henry said firmly.

"Who?" Emma asked.

"The leader of the Northern Anarchy Corps. She's built quite the group up here," Henry said.

"Who is she?"

"Sheena Edwards," Brynn said.

AGENTS OF THE DESERT

Acknowledgements

Hey Everyone!

Thank you for taking the time to read *Agents of the Desert*. I really hoped you enjoyed reading it as much as I did writing it. This wouldn't have happened without some really great people, so I wanted to take a quick moment to thank them.

First up is my sister Cheryl. By default she's my biggest fan, but she has been absolutely instrumental in getting this thing into print. She encouraged me through the writing process by texting me things like "Yay!", "Can't wait to read it!" and "You're awesome!". Post writing, she has been more than invaluable to my editing process. Her love of reading has helped me delve deeper into the literary world and I can't thank her enough.

Next, Mike Wing, my cover guy. His keen artistic eye has helped bring to life the cover art that hopefully attracted you to this book. An award winning gifted photographer and graphic designer, Mike is an all-around fantastic guy to work with and is always quick to come up with the perfect idea to make the artwork

that much better. Check out some of his work at: https://www.
mikewing.photo

Finally, I'd like to thank my late grandmother, Hazel. She was
immensely proud of me for writing *Insurgent Fire* and it saddens
me that she's unable to read this one. I know in my heart that
she would be just as proud. Love you, Grams!

ABOUT THE AUTHOR

D.S. Cannon is a former Canadian Forces member and a veteran of the conflict in Afghanistan. He served as a reservist with the Princess of Wales Own Regiment and then with the Third Battalion – Royal Canadian Regiment in Afghanistan. He retired from military service in 2013 a year after completing his post-secondary education and moved onto working in the administration field. Writing started for him as a cathartic method to ease stress and anxiety. He had never dreamed it would blossom into something more.